THE BATTLE OF ZOMBIE HILL

THE BATTLE OF ZOMBIE HILL

DEFENDERS OF THE OVERWORLD

BOOK 1

Nancy Osa

61 Biomes . . . 6 Friends . . . 1 World

Sky Pony Press
New York

Copyright © 2015 by Hollan Publishing, Inc.

First Edition

This is a work of fiction. Names, characters, places, and incidents are from the author's
imagination, and used fictitiously.

Sky Pony Press books may be purchased in bulk at special discounts for sales pro-
motion, corporate gifts, fund-raising, or educational purposes. Special editions
can also be created to specifications. For details, contact the Special Sales Depart-
ment, Sky Pony Press, 307 West 36th Street, 11th Floor, New York, NY 10018 or
info@skyhorsepublishing.com.

Sky Pony® is a registered trademark of Skyhorse Publishing, Inc.®,
a Delaware corporation.

Minecraft® is a registered trademark of Notch Development AB.
The Minecraft game is copyright © Mojang AB.

Visit our website at www.skyponypress.com.

10 9 8 7 6 5 4 3 2 1

Library of Congress Cataloging-in-Publication Data on file.

Cover illustration by Stephanie Hazel Evans
Cover design by Brian Peterson

Print ISBN: 978-1-63450-996-1
Ebook ISBN: 978-1-63450-998-5

Printed in Canada

For my miner and redstone friends at
Reynolds Learning Academy,
Nick, Sean, and Colton
. . . and for Ken, Marc, and Charles

THE BATTLE OF ZOMBIE HILL

The cavalry commander watched the last of his troops hurry into the hidden Nether portal with their horses. The ragged soldiers had come such a long way from their days as solo players. How had they reached this point? Now a trip to the Nether was safer than a moonlight trail ride.

It had been the wildest night ride of Roberto's life. What had begun as a snap, a cinch—a midnight run, for goodness sake—had become a massacre. Diamond-armored zombies, enchanted skeletons, and immortal griefers had forced his battalion into a stranglehold, putting their artilleryman and the villagers in mortal danger. It had been his decision to ride uphill, and now there was no way down. One wrong move would have been the end of them all.

At the last moment, Rob had to cut his losses to prevent any more bloodshed. Fleeing the Overworld, he realized, might be the only way to someday save it. As much as Rob pined for his home, this place deserved to be released from griefer tyranny and the people free to go where they would. Stormie had shown him that.

Rob led Saber toward the Nether portal and took one last look at the sky, all purple-black, aglow with twinkling stars. He might not be of this world, but he was in it. And he would defend it . . . wherever that might take him.

CHAPTER 1

ONE MOMENT ROB WAS LEAFING THROUGH THE in-flight magazine, glad to be returning home to the ranch—and the next, he was falling. Something had gone terribly wrong with the plane. But where was he now . . . ?

And where were the other passengers?

Although he had never fallen from thirty thousand feet before, that was clearly what was happening.

I should be more afraid, he thought as he plummeted through the spotty cloud cover. The land below unfolded like a map: blue ocean bordered by white sand, a stripe of green trees. And—beyond—swaths of open meadow broken by rock formations. His face dampened as he caught the tail end of a rainstorm and then instantly dried as he dropped through the atmosphere, heading for the ever-looming landscape

1

below. He was going to fall into the chunky waves, he realized.

Suddenly, debilitating fear knifed through him. Gravity drew his body downward at a speed he had never experienced before, even at the fastest gallop. His desperate screams disintegrated into thin air— perhaps because there was no one else to hear them. As the shifting blue floor rose up to swallow him, Rob felt, rather than heard, the all-encompassing splash. Down, down, down he plunged, his brain churning up a final, if useless, thought: *Travel ain't all it's cracked up to be.*

*

Wicked fear, the impact, and a lack of oxygen had caused Rob to blackout, but it couldn't have been for long. When next he was aware of his body, he was still underwater, surprised to be alive. That shock activated his arms and legs, and he began kicking and flailing his way back to the surface. Something brushed against his rib cage, and he felt a long, gelatinous body swipe past. *What the heck was that?* he wondered, then answered his own question with a vague memory from science class: a squid!

The next thing Rob knew, he had popped above the churning waterline and was coughing and gulping in air. He couldn't pause to concentrate on breathing, though. As soon as he stopped kicking, he began to sink. Instinctively, he resumed swimming, hauling in ragged breaths until his heart stopped feeling like an exploding boulder. Through watery eyes, he peered in all directions, seeing nothing but rolling blocks of liquid. He figured he had two choices: panic or don't.

He summoned up the worst scenario he had ever faced—riding a bucking bronco through a nest of rattlesnakes—and decided to do now what he had done then. *Just stay alive,* he told himself. *Best focus on the job at hand.*

Rob rolled over and noted the position of the sun in the sky, resolving to swim in the opposite direction until he found help. He had lost his cowboy hat and boots, but still wore his chaps, shirt, and vest, which now clung to his body. *Funny, this water seems warm, too. No, just . . . not cold.* At least hypothermia wouldn't add to his woes. He continued to make his way through the tepid waves, away from the sun, which was just past its high point in the sky.

Minute after minute he pushed himself on. Every now and then, he flipped over to rest on his back for a count of ten, then resumed his slow but steady progress. *But progress toward what? Anything at all?*

He wondered if there were sharks, stingrays, or other animal mobs in this version of the world.

Would there be dry land, a boat, or some other form of rescue?

As recent events had reminded him, he would only find out what came next by encountering it.

*

Stroke after stroke, Rob cut through the ocean chunks, thoughts of his home on the range spurring him on. The water gradually cooled as day slipped toward dusk, and he wondered if he would have to spend the night at sea—cold, hungry, and tired. Could he survive that?

"*Can't* never could do anything," he muttered. He resolved to stay positive, no matter how bleak the horizon might look.

He rolled over onto his back to rest for ten seconds and to ensure he was still swimming in the right direction. It felt so good to float. *Maybe an extra second or two won't hurt,* he thought, admiring the deepening palette of the sky, which had turned bronze and taken on pink and purple tinges. The extra rest made it harder to flip over and resume paddling, though he forced himself to do so.

In the distance, a white stripe appeared to seal off the ocean. Was he seeing things? Gathering his fading strength, Rob pulled himself up on the next stroke and gasped. It *was* land!

Relief, excitement, and desperation surged through him, propelling his limbs ever faster in an attempt to reach the end of today's rainbow. But hours of swimming had taken their toll. Rob could barely feel his fingers or toes. *And I'm so hungry,* he thought. Luckily, he didn't know how low his food bar was. He pushed harder, his shortened strokes barely inching him through the surf. But at last he saw breakwater. The beach was real! He would be safe for the night.

Once in the shallows, Rob half-stood and half-crawled his way to shore. The ordeal was over. He would live.

He lay on the sand gasping like a fish, thinking he had never seen a more beautiful sunset.

*

The cool air dried the last drops of seawater from his shock of black hair but left his clothes damp. Rob slowly rose from the beach and staggered in a circle. The dunes stretched inland quite a ways, but he could see square tufts jutting upward in the distance—trees—a forest or jungle of some kind. *There'll be food and water there.* But he knew he didn't have the energy to cover any more distance that day. The sun's light was fading, and all he wanted now was to stop moving and sink into a deep, sound sleep.

Even so, the prospect of dozing on the open beach made Rob nervous. Any cowpoke worth his salt knew to cover his back at night, preferably beside a nice, warm campfire. He scanned the empty shoreline. Not a scrap of burnable driftwood or even dried seaweed in sight, and the open expanse offered no natural shelter. Rob was on his own. He smiled. Solitude had its pros and cons; at least there was nobody to bother him.

Still, he considered it a good idea to sleep up off the ground, if he could. The only resource around was sand, and plenty of it. So he decided to pile some up to form a shelf. That would get him off the ground and ward off . . . whatever needed warding.

But as he started handling the sand, he found that it wasn't loose the way it was back home in the dry gulch. He couldn't push it into a tower. In fact, it was already held together in neat blocks. Maybe he could stack the stuff into a pillar?

His days of performing tricks with a lasso on the ranch had made Rob a good jumper. With nearly the last of his strength, he leapt up in the air, grabbed a block of sand, and settled on top of it. For good measure, he placed a second sand block beneath his feet just as the sun dove below the horizon.

"Now I can catch some z's," he said, and the next moment he did.

But it wasn't long before a strange noise woke him.

"Uuuuh . . . oooh . . ."

The low moaning was like nothing Rob had ever heard on the ranch—not the lowing of a cow in distress or the whining of his favorite dog, Jip.

"Uuh-oohhhh . . ."

The otherworldly groan seemed to pierce the air. Rob's eyelids felt like concrete and had crusted shut with salt and sand—but he forced them open. As his vision cleared, he made out a shape coming toward him in the dark. The groaning grew louder as the creature approached in a jerky shuffle that sent Rob's heart knocking into his teeth. He sat straight up on his sand pillar. The intruder spied him and increased its pace.

It's still a ways off, Rob reasoned. *Maybe I can build this tower up a little higher before it gets here.* His body was heavy with sleep and weak from hunger and thirst, but Rob managed to pillar jump and add another block of sand beneath his feet. Still, the bellowing creature came closer.

In the moonlight reflected from the ocean surface, Rob could make out a green form that looked human, but sure didn't act like it . . . and acted, but sure didn't look, alive. He sniffed the air and retched at an odor not unlike the inside of his neglected refrigerator back home. With less juice than usual flowing to his brain, it took Rob a while to recognize the sunken eyes, decomposing flesh, and lurching gait as signs of the undead.

Every zombie flick he'd ever watched came flooding back to him.

A zombie! The thing stunk like a science experiment. And there was nowhere to run.

The flailing monster clearly wanted Rob: to rip his limbs off; kill him; or—worst of all—turn him into one of its own kind. Rob didn't know whether the hideous thing could reach him three blocks up or not . . . and he didn't want to find out. Alone, afraid, and weaponless, Rob would be at the zombie's mercy if it decided to attack. It wasn't something a good cowboy would do, but Rob squeezed his eyes shut tight and waited for the end.

The noise of the zombie's cries and lumbering advance had covered the movements of another visitor. When, at last, Rob cracked open an eye, he was shocked to find a second two-legged enemy already at the foot of his pillar. Its mottled, green skin was intact, but its eyes and mouth bulged huge and dark. Rob had seen nothing in the movies like this.

"Go on, get out of here!" he shouted, as though he were back on the range, trying to scare off a coyote.

His cry had no effect. For a brief instant, he hoped the two intruders would fight it out between themselves. But, to his horror, the one that had crept up unseen began to quiver and hiss loudly. The zombie ignored the creeper, trying in vain to swipe at Rob, who still crouched on his tiny island of sand just above the demon's head. The creeper began flashing pulses of light in the darkness, and Rob saw it inflate to twice its size.

He gulped bile. *This is it!* he thought, preparing to die.

Then the thing exploded with a deafening *boom*.

Rob was just high enough to escape harm from the blast, but his relief at not being blown to smithereens lasted exactly a nanosecond. Once again he felt himself falling helplessly, right toward the hideous zombie!

At least the creeper had taken itself out along with Rob's makeshift bedroom. Sand flew in every direction as the homemade pillar fell apart. The castaway cowboy seemed to fall in slow motion in a descent every bit as drawn out as the one from the airplane that had spawned him into this deadly zone. He had plenty of time to dread his end.

Finally, he thudded to the ground. *"Oof!"*

He waited. There was no answering moan.

His arms and legs were still attached to his body.

He wasn't dead.

And—he made a quick mental check—he was pretty sure he wasn't a zombie.

Yet, Rob had suffered some injuries and could barely move. In the dim moonlight, he saw the sand pile—all that remained of his pillar. Suddenly it shifted. Something was writhing underneath.

Rob sprang back as a muffled groan accompanied another bump from the pile of sand. Then the ground was still; the moaning abruptly ended. The falling sand must have suffocated the zombie.

Disturbing the body was the last thing Rob wanted to do. But he had to know for certain that the zombie had been neutralized. Just like old Jip, he crawled on his belly and began pawing the pile to unearth the rotten corpse. To his intense relief, it moved no more. He was about to abandon the pile when he felt a small, hard item in the sand. A few more scoops revealed a long, triangular object—a carrot! The zombie had dropped the vegetable when it expired.

Misfortune turned to luck, and Rob hastily crammed half of the raw carrot into his mouth and chewed, his food bar and health improving by an increment. If he had been able to start a fire and come up with some beef, he would have cooked a stew for greater benefit, but the carrot was a start. He felt better, stronger. Maybe he would survive the night after all.

Just as he was starting to relax, a wave of groans floated toward him. "Uuuuh, oooh . . . !"

More zombies? The monster must have called on its friends for help before being completely suffocated by sand.

This time, Rob knew what to do. There was no telling what other hostile mobs were out there in the gloom, coming his way—or what their powers might be. With his remaining strength, he'd have to rebuild his pillar better and higher.

He worked into the night, clumsily digging down through the sand until he hit natural sandstone. *Eureka!* These blocks would make a more stable foundation that could withstand damage, though probably not an explosion. Rob hoped he wouldn't be visited by another creeper tonight.

He dug, placed, jumped, and stacked, until he stood atop a sand pillar twelve blocks high. The sandstone at the base created a solid platform. Rob felt confident that whatever might be lurking out in the darkness wouldn't be able to scale his new sand tower.

He sneaked a look over the side of his structure.

Nothing.

But, just to be safe, he'd stay awake a while longer to keep watch.

*

Rob crouched on his pillar, munching the other half of his carrot and hoping dawn would arrive before anything else did. What had seemed unimportant this morning had now become critical. He wished he had the knife he always carried with him back home. He should have eaten that bag of food on the plane. He should have brought his bedroll—he could've used it to keep off the chill. But, most of all, he should've have paid more attention to where he was as he fell from the sky. Yep, the things he had taken for granted before could help him stay alive now. . . . At least long enough to find his way home.

A sharp pang of loneliness cut through him.

He started humming the little tune he always sang to Jip before leaving him in his doghouse for the night. Then Rob thought about the foal he'd just started training to lead and the pony he had broke to saddle. He wondered if he would ever see them or his beloved ranch again. Back home, the air smelled sweet, not salty like the beachfront here. On the range there was plenty of room to roam, but he'd never felt vulnerable like he did here, even twelve blocks up above the ground. Most of all, life on the ranch was peaceful— he'd fall asleep to the chirping of crickets, the bay of a lone coyote, or the low of a wayward cow, not to groans and explosions and toppling pillars of sand.

He sighed.

Then he blew out a more determined breath. One that meant business.

"I *will* go home again," he vowed, buoyed by the sound of his own voice. "I survived the plane crash, I survived being adrift in the ocean, and I survived two dangerous monster attacks." He balled up his fists. "I'll do whatever it takes to get back to the ranch!"

He curled up on top of his sandy bed and drifted off to sleep.

*

Although Rob heard moaning in the night, he was so exhausted that he didn't get up. He knew he had done all he could to safeguard himself.

Toward morning, a rank odor poked at his nostrils, making him toss on his pillar. But he was unprepared for what he saw.

The zombie mob had arrived. They milled about below the pillar, their undead eyes searching for Rob. As the sun's rays crept over the horizon, the zombies tried to take cover in the shade cast by the tower, but the sun was not high enough to produce any shadows. Rob watched as the gang of monsters burst into flame: *Poom! Poom! Poom!* They shook and crackled and sizzled before finally burning up and disappearing.

Awesome! Rob pumped his fist a few times, feeling like he was in a movie himself. Then his stomach growled. *Maybe they've left more carrots I can eat,* he thought, scrambling down from his sandy perch.

But when he reached the beach, all he found were a few mounds of rotten flesh. "Ugh! Disgusting!" He wouldn't even feed such slop to Jip. Rob left the junk on the sand and set out to find the tree line he'd spied yesterday. At least he remembered one landmark that might be useful.

Rob crunched over the dunes as the sun rose, casting a warm glow on his shoulders. It made him think of the sunny days he'd spent riding fences on the ranch, whistling to one of his horses as Jip trotted along beside them. Maybe across the line of trees he would find the mountainous region he'd spotted from the air yesterday. He wished he could recall what direction it had been, but there was no use crying over spilt milk. . . . *Mmmm, milk,* he thought, savoring the idea of a warm drink, fresh from the cow.

Lost in his daydreams, he nearly missed a strange sign. Placing his foot in a depression in the sand, he did a double take. The hollow spot was the exact shape of his foot! It was unmistakably a footprint—someone *else's* footprint.

Rob's chest tightened with hope and fear. A footprint could be *good* if it meant he'd found a friendly person who could help him. But it could *suck* if that person were an enemy who wished him harm. Still, it could be good if he were able to secretly follow that person to resources or food he could use. . . . Yet, it could be extremely sucky if it belonged to a member of a hostile mob.

Rob quickly hunted for a matching footprint or signs of others having passed this way. There were none. "Who the heck leaves a single footprint?" he wondered aloud, fear winning his battle of emotions.

He felt more exposed than ever on the lonely stretch of beach. He crouched, glancing over both shoulders. Then he pushed off from the sand and sprinted as fast as he could for the tree line in the distance.

CHAPTER 2

THE COPSE OF LEAFY, GREEN TREES WAS EVEN farther away than Rob had thought. Running used up his body's fuel, and his food bar depleted. He slowed to a jog, then a shuffle, then a crawl. He stopped and listened a moment. Paranoia swept over him. It was quiet . . . too quiet. He could be wrong, but it felt as though someone were watching him from the trees. Yet he saw nothing but plant life and heard nothing but the ocean waves breaking onshore behind him.

It seemed strange not to hear the calls of birds or even the buzzing of flies, the way he would have in his world. "I'm definitely not on the range anymore," he murmured sleepily, not realizing how close he was to both starvation and salvation. The empty sands had created a mirage—not of a fabulous oasis, but of more

17

empty sand stretching before him. The vision threatened to pop Rob's bubble of hope. Would he never reach the lush trees?

The answer literally slapped him in the face.

Wham! The cowboy collided face-first with a tree trunk. He slumped to the ground and then felt a second, smaller impact. An apple had been jarred loose and fallen, tapping his shoulder before rolling a few blocks away.

Rob groggily recognized the fruit, crawled forward, and grabbed it, cramming it into his mouth, seeds and all. His food bar refilled ever so slightly. As he finished the apple, Rob got to his feet.

He looked up. Foliage towered above him, vines cascaded down tree trunks. The oak tree that had stopped him in his tracks was one of several that grew in the area. Between the jungle treetops, the morning sky appeared faded, while down on the biome floor, it was shady. The sun's rays filtered through the dark green gloom. In the ominous silence, Rob could almost hear someone—or *something*—watching him.

He shook off the feeling and concentrated on exploring his new environment. Where there was one apple, there might be more. *I'd rather not pick them with my face, though,* Rob thought, rubbing the spot where he'd been hit.

He punched at one of the trees, and some wood dropped, though no fruit. He put two of the wood planks together and formed a stick. *Perfect!* He. whacked at the leaves and was rewarded with two apples falling to the ground. He quickly ate one and saved the other in his inventory for later, along with the stick. He had a feeling he was going to need them.

Standing around in the semidarkness wasn't going to get him any closer to home, so he set off through the trees. The going was slow over the leaf-strewn ground. Rob didn't know what he was looking for, but as he walked, a plan began to take shape in his mind.

"What I need to do is get to a vantage point," he said to himself. "Get up high, get the lay of the land. Maybe then I'll be able to find my way out of here or at least find somebody who knows where I am." He was unaware that he was moving farther away from his spawn point every minute.

But the apple had restored his spirits along with his health. He hummed a little under his breath as he plowed through the brush, hoping to reach a break in the tree cover. Yet, even with his positive mood, the sensation of unseen eyes following him was unnerving.

At last Rob came upon a small clearing in the bush trees, where only gigantic jungle trunks held up the canopy overhead. He was surprised to see a square of stone blocks, obviously not natural. Cautiously, he approached, half expecting some demon to shoot out at him. But nothing blocked his progress toward the open doorway.

Rob peeked inside. There lay another carrot. A guy couldn't have too much food, he figured, so he entered and reached for the edible prize . . . and a door slammed shut behind him.

Not only was he trapped, but as he turned the root vegetable around in his hand, he realized that it was just a triangular wood block dyed to resemble a carrot. He'd been duped. And he had no idea what the person—or *thing*—that had corralled him was going to do with him.

*

"Surrender your supplies, griefer!" came a harsh voice that sent chills up Rob's spine.

The next second, he felt some of the tension roll away. His captor was human. Still, Rob was smart enough to hang on to the only possessions he had. "No way!" he yelled.

"Then I'll have to kill you. . . ."

The door swung open. There stood a girl, her hair tucked up beneath a brown leather cap. Her olive green skin and camouflage outfit blended in with the flora behind her. She wielded a large sword, which reflected the low jungle light when she moved.

Rob backed away as she advanced into the stone trap. He peered into the corners but saw no cover, and gritted his teeth as she stepped toward him, brandishing the sword above her head. Then, without warning, the girl collapsed, her sword flying toward him, and she hit the ground.

Rob grabbed the weapon but could not imagine using it on another person. "Are you all right?" he asked.

The girl's eyelids fluttered, but she didn't seem to see him. "So . . . weak," she muttered. "So hungry . . ."

Indeed, she appeared to be near death. Rob rummaged in his inventory and produced the apple and gave it to her, hoping it would be enough.

She ate, and her vision returned. She watched Rob from beneath her leather cap, sizing him up, trying to decide whether he was a threat. "What do you want with me, griefer?" she finally said.

"N-nothing," Rob answered. "Otherwise, why would I give you my last apple? And what's a—? I don't even know what a *griefer* is."

She looked unconvinced.

"Uh, here's your sword." He held out the weapon. She grabbed it and jumped to her feet, her energy having surged back with the small meal.

"Explain yourself, stranger!" she commanded, backing Rob into a corner.

He doubted that his stick would be a match for her sword, so he dropped it, too, in a gesture of surrender. "I'm . . . lost." Maybe honesty would save his skin right now.

The girl snorted. "You're an idiot!" She swiped the stick and put it in her own inventory. "I've been watching you all day. You're wasteful, you're slow, and you're not too bright. You walked right into my trap!"

Rob couldn't argue with that. In fact, he had to admire her clever decoy. "A fake carrot," he said, tossing the wooden vegetable in her direction. "What were you trying to do, tame a wooden rabbit?"

She caught it and added it to her inventory as well. "Yeah. A big, dumb one. And I have to say, buddy, you're about as helpless as a fluffy bunny."

Rob's stomach churned. He was not used to being defenseless, much less called dumb by a girl. "Hey, I told you I'm lost. I was lucky to survive the night. Did you know there're zombies loose around here?"

"Well, duh," she retorted. "What were you doing out at night? Of course, you're not doing so great during the day, either. You wasted all kinds of food and supplies. I had to pick up the rotten flesh and gunpowder that the zombies and creeper dropped when they died so it wouldn't go to waste. But then it made me sick."

"R-rotten flesh?" Rob repeated. "And I didn't see any gunpowder."

"It was mixed in with the sand. Look, what's your name? That way I'll know what to put on your tombstone."

"I'm Roberto. You can call me Rob. What about you?"

She eyed him, unsure whether to trust him or not. These were the very tactics employed by griefers. But there was something innocent about this player. "Well . . . you did give me your apple. Which was stupid!"

He nodded.

"They call me Frida."

"Who does?"

"The people who matter," she said. "Listen, there are griefers all over the place. That's how I ended up so hungry. I had to sprint forever just to cross over the last biome boundary to get away from them. It was heavily guarded by skeletons." She shuddered. "I might never leave the jungle again."

This roused Rob's curiosity. "What's the next biome over? I'm trying to find a really high hill. Or some mountains."

"Are you out of your mind? You'll never get there. Not with Dr. Dirt's armies in the way."

Armies? That didn't sound good.

"Look, pal—er, Rob." Frida's voice softened as she moved away. "You want to stay alive? You'd better stick with me. At least until you learn how to take care of yourself in this version of the Overworld."

"Um, thanks, Frida. Don't mind if I do."

*

The two acquaintances spent the rest of the afternoon gathering and storing items that Frida said they'd need. She crafted a chest and placed it in the small stone enclosure, telling Rob what to put in it. She showed him how to make a wooden axe for chopping wood and how to use the axe as a weapon. "Until you get something stronger, it's better than nothing." Rob heartily agreed.

They crept through the jungle, chatting as they worked.

"Who's this Dr. Dirt?" Rob asked.

"More like, *what* is he?" Frida hacked away at a mass of vines with her own stone axe. "He's a griefer. No—he's the king of the griefers. They're masters of deception. They act all sweet, fish you in, and then, *bam!* They steal your resources or burn your house down. Dr. Dirt commands a whole slew of them. And they've somehow enchanted hostile mobs. Dirt's that powerful. Believe me, you don't want to meet him.

And you won't, if you stay in this biome and keep to yourself." Her axe broke, and she groaned.

Like lightning, she crafted herself a new one, using Rob's stick and a piece of iron she had in her inventory. "That's my last iron ingot!" She sighed, then returned to the cowboy's question. "Griefers took most of my supplies. Dr. Dirt and his underlings control the skeleton mobs and are using them as shields while they take whatever they can find from whoever they can find."

Rob's head was spinning. *Thieves and walking skeletons, not to mention zombies and exploding creepers!* There sure was a lot of danger to watch out for in this world. "Then why not get as far away from these griefers as possible? Like, the next biome over?"

"Tried that." She rooted around in some ferns for useful items. "Dr. Dirt is commanding the skeletons to attack travelers at every biome boundary I've come across. They're armed and dangerous." Then she cried, "Woohoo!" and backed out of the thicket. "A melon block!"

As Rob watched, she busted up the block into half a dozen melons. They each ate one immediately. Rob spit out the seeds.

"Don't do that!" Frida scolded. "We can plant them later. Listen, Rob. First rule of survival: Don't waste anything!" She saw his clueless expression and cracked a small smile. "Even if you don't know how you can use it."

They each ate another melon and then put the extras and the seeds in the chest. "It's good to have a stash here," Frida told him, "in case we have to hole up for a while."

"You mean, this isn't your home?"

"Heck, no!" she said. "These low walls wouldn't keep a spider out. But I ran out of cobblestone when I was building it." She glanced up at the sky through the trees. "Yikes. We'd better be heading back to my place. It's getting dark."

"And that's when the zombies come out," Rob said with a shiver.

Frida looked at him. "That's when the zombies come out," she echoed. "You're getting it, pardner."

Rob felt like he'd learned something for the first time since he landed in the ocean. It was supremely satisfying. Plus, he'd have somewhere to sleep for the night.

Frida took off through the jungle. "Follow me!"

Rob hurried to keep up. He noticed a tiny tattoo of an apple with an arrow through it on the back of her neck and used it to pick her out among the greenery. In his old life, he had often gone days without seeing another soul while riding fences, but now, spending a night alone was the last thing he wanted to do.

"So, where're you from?" Frida asked over her shoulder, as though reading Rob's thoughts.

He paused. "I used to tell people I was from the West, but now I'm not so sure anymore. Yesterday I fell out of the sky."

"Then it's going to be awfully tough to get back to your spawn point. You'll probably have to find an enchanted portal or just die to get back there."

"Oh, I'm dying to get back there," he assured her, knowing nothing about spawn points. "Back home to my ranch. What I was thinking is, if I got up on a high point someplace, I could get a better idea of where I am and where I came from. See, I was on my way back from vacation when my plane went down—or went somewhere." He had never actually seen it go down, but he thought that a vantage point might give him some clue as to what had happened.

"Well, you're not going to find anything high enough to help you around here," Frida said, "and getting to the extreme hills is going to be way too dangerous. You'd have to cross several boundaries, and Dr. Dirt's armies are running amok between here and there."

"So? We'll find a way." Rob sounded determined.

Frida stopped short. "What do you mean, 'we'?"

"Well, you seem pretty brave."

"Brave, yes. Stupid, no." She wheeled around again and picked up the pace. "Cowboy, let's go!" she called. "We're burning daylight."

They hustled on, stopping only briefly to add fallen apples to their supplies.

Rob hadn't traveled this far on foot since . . . ever. "How much farther is it to your house?" he asked.

"Cave," she corrected. "It's just over that—" She pointed to a rise, and then grunted when something hit her from above. She sagged as the weight of a full-grown human landing on her shoulders pulled her to the ground. The creature let loose a bloodcurdling yell: *"Aaaughhh!"*

Rob jumped back, watching helplessly while the intruder raked at Frida's head with its arms and gouged at her sides with its legs. Her leather cap protected her head, but her unarmored sides took a beating. With a leap, she threw the man off and began showering him with debris: leaves, dirt, even precious apples. This gave her enough time to reach into her inventory for her sword. She fumbled and bent down to grab it. Her assailant was too quick, blocking her arm, then splashing her with a potion of slowness. Now her sword was even more unob-tainable . . . to her.

Rob watched—horrified—as her attacker reached down and retrieved the weapon. He stepped menacingly toward Frida, and Rob noticed his muscular arms and heavily tattooed skin. He knew he should do something to stop this maniac, but what?

Thinking fast, he made a loud *click* sound and stuck a finger in the man's back. "Drop it and reach for the sky!"

To Rob's surprise, the muscle-bound man did just that. Rob hesitated a moment, shocked that his ploy had worked, then recovered Frida's sword. "Are you okay?" he asked his new friend.

She nodded slowly. "It'll wear . . . off . . . soon."

Nobody moved.

Then Frida said to her assailant, "You . . . win. You've got . . . one . . . on me." She turned in slow motion to Rob, and a grin spread across her lips. "Rob: Meet my friend . . . Turner."

*

Soon the spell had worn off. Frida explained to Rob that she and Turner had an ongoing rivalry—whenever they met, they each tried to out-ambush the other. The two were laughing and joking as they continued on their way across the jungle floor, Rob trailing behind them. He was put off by their behavior—if that's how friends greeted each other around here, he sure didn't want to make any enemies.

"Turner here keeps me sharp," Frida said, referring to the surprise attack. "That was a good one, Meat."

Turner seemed to take the nickname as a compliment. "Same to you," he replied. "Survivalists have to do all we can to stay alert, sharp, and strong." He looked the part, with his cargo pants, ripped T-shirt, and buzz-cut hair.

"Especially in the jungle," Frida added. "Mobs can spawn here in the daytime in the dimmest areas. Glad we didn't meet any today."

"Me, too," Rob agreed.

"Or what?" Turner challenged. "You would've told 'em to reach?"

Frida laughed at Rob's reddening cheeks. She punched him lightly. "Seriously, dude. Does that work where you come from?"

"Yeah, well . . ."

"Nice try, anyway," Turner said.

Rob was glad to have their company as dusk fell.

CHAPTER 3

THE THREE TRAVELERS REACHED FRIDA'S CAVERN just as moans, groans, skitters, and rattles filled the air.

"Get inside!" Frida shouted.

They followed her into a cave fortified with cobblestone and an iron door at the entrance. Frida slammed the door shut behind them, pitching the cave into darkness.

Then she crafted two torches, illuminating the cave walls and revealing a large, black spider. It sprang toward Rob. Before his reflexes could respond, Turner eliminated the beast with a stone axe.

"Thanks, man!"

Turner nodded.

Frida checked the arachnid body. "At least it wasn't poisonous."

"It must have followed us in from outside," Turner said as he scooped up the string the spider had dropped. "Just what I need. I'm making weapons tonight."

"Then you're going to want what's in my basement," Frida said, motioning for Turner and Rob to follow her.

At the end of the small cave vestibule was a staircase. Frida quarried into the wall and pulled out some coal, which she used to form several more torches to light their way. They descended through layers until they arrived at the bottom, where the cavern opened into a large great room. Rob was surprised at how cozy it looked. There was a bed, a fireplace, a wool rug, and another chest, which Frida approached and began to rummage in.

She tossed a piece of wool to Turner and one to Rob. "You can sleep on that."

A bedroll! Rob thought. This was beginning to feel like home.

But Turner declined the offer. "Trying to change my spawn point, eh, Frida? My spawn coordinates are a secret, and I mean to keep them that way."

She shrugged. "Up to you." She bent over and lit the furnace. "Got any meat?" she asked Turner, causing Rob to drool a little bit.

"Don't I always?" Turner threw three hams in to cook. "We can use the same fire to craft some armor after we eat."

"Why armor?" Rob asked. "This place seems safe from attack."

"I'm low on all kinds of resources," Frida said, "and we'll have to cross the jungle boundary if we want to trade with the villagers." She looked at Turner. "I'm assuming that's why you're here."

"Right. I need supplies, too. And don't underestimate Dr. Dirt's skeletons."

"I have an axe," Rob offered, glad to have one weapon in his arsenal.

Turner and Frida exchanged glances. "You don't want to get in close when you're fighting skeletons," Frida told the cowboy.

Turner flipped the grilling ham on its other side, and a rich aroma filled the enclosed space. "I recommend at least an iron chest plate and a bow and arrow—preferably several of each, in case some break. That will let you keep your distance but still meet fire with fire."

Frida saw Rob's blank stare. "Skeletons. Shoot arrows," she prompted, then sighed. "Yikes, Rob. What you don't know would fill a book." She swiveled toward Turner and added, "He's new here. He's lost. He's a babe in the woods."

Turner grinned. "I can see that. But how did you two meet?"

Rob and Frida pieced together their encounter and the events leading up to it, then explained his plan to trek to the extreme hills to find his way home.

"Phee-ew!" Turner sighed. "Frida, you escaped from one of Dirt's skeleton platoons on foot?" He regarded Rob with reserved respect. "And you fell out of the sky and spent your first night on a sand pillar? Even for a newbie, that's pretty darn good."

"What about you, Meat?" Frida asked. "How did you make it to my section of the jungle?"

Her friend let out a long breath. "It was pretty hairy. I was taken in by one of Dirt's top griefers. Guy by the name of Legs. He told me he could get me the diamonds I wanted in exchange for my help crafting a cage. Once I built it, though, he used a potion of weakness on me and sent in a file of zombies to attack me."

Hearing the name of the monsters made Rob cringe. Still, he had to know: "What happened next?"

Turner chuckled. "I had a high-level healing potion in my inventory to counteract the spell. I went after Legs, but the zombies surrounded him like an undead fence. I couldn't get at him without getting to them, and if I battled them, he would've had a chance to hit me with something else from his bag of tricks." Turner paused. "I guess you could call it a draw. But then a wave of skeletons marched in, and I didn't stick around to skirmish."

"How'd you run into that bunch?" Frida asked.

"I was just minding my own business, looking for bodyguard work, when I crossed over the cold taiga boundary. Legs appeared, saying he wanted to trap a wild wolf and needed a cage. I figured I'd make a few diamonds off the job and keep moving, but that's when the grit hit the fan."

"And they attacked you," Rob concluded, recalling how Frida had lured him into her trap. At least she had been acting to defend herself, not trying to con him.

"That's creepy," Frida said. "Dr. Dirt's legions are as far out as the cold taiga? I met them at the plains and mesa boundaries."

Rob guessed that these zones lay between the jungle and the extreme hills. Not good. "It's like this guy is trying to take over the world!" he said.

Turner narrowed his eyes. "Take over the Overworld is more like it."

*

The three debated the topic as they ate their ham.

"What do you think the odds are of Dr. Dirt managing to infiltrate every world boundary?" Frida asked.

Turner folded his arms. "It would be pretty tough. There are more than sixty biomes, with double or triple the boundaries."

Frida frowned. "This is going to cause havoc for villagers across the grid. Trading is about to get tricky."

Turner spoke through a mouthful of ham. "Just making a living is about to get tricky. I have to cross a boundary at a moment's notice. It's my stock-in-trade." He swallowed and held out his arms, which were covered with the ink drawings that Rob had noticed earlier.

"What are they?" he asked.

"Each one represents a biome that I've explored," Turner said smugly. "I make my gems protecting other people's valuables from mobs and griefers." He deflated a bit. "Only now, my credibility ain't so hot."

Rob worried. If this leatherneck had been taken in by a griefer, what chance did he have?

Frida's eyes moved from Turner's to Rob's. "There's safety in numbers," she said quietly.

Turner wasn't sure he'd heard her right. "You mean, this guy—?"

Frida put a hand on Rob's shoulder. "He's green, but he's got spunk."

"We're gonna need a lot more than spunk," Turner said dryly.

Rob thought back to his world, where his skills had been more than sufficient to survive on the range. "I've got way more than, er, spunk," he assured them. "I can rope, mend fence, round up cattle, and gentle even the wildest bucking bronco."

"That all sounds so sweet." Turner shook his head. "But I think I'll do better on my own."

Frida stepped in. "Ah, give him a chance, Meat. Some of the stuff he can do might come in handy."

Turner considered this a moment. "Well . . . all right. But if I take an arrow because of him, I'm cutting you two loose."

They finished up their meal and sat around the furnace relaxing. Frida's basement stronghold was well fortified. They could hear banging on the iron door above, but nothing penetrated it.

"I can see why you wouldn't want to leave this place," Rob said, admiring the homey chamber.

His host shrugged. "Oh, it's just temporary. Sooner or later something or someone will find a way in. A girl doesn't stay alive in the jungle for long by sticking in one spot. I'll probably mine this out and move on."

"But what about safety in numbers?"

"For traveling to villages, yeah," Frida said. "Otherwise, I'm pretty much a loner."

Turner started lining up items from his inventory. "When it comes to resources, Newbie, we're all in competition." He eyed Frida, who had risen to search for something in her supply chest. "It's a friendly rivalry," he continued, "but it's still a rivalry."

"Second that." She backed away from the chest and threw Turner three sticks she'd taken from a stack. "Can I have some of that spider string?"

"You got it." He tossed her a ball of it, and they got down to crafting bows.

Rob still licked his fingers, savoring the cooked meat taste as long as possible. He tried to understand Frida and Turner's relationship. Out in the wild, they—and others like them, he supposed—competed for food and raw materials. Here inside the shelter, though, they helped each other out. They even shared a crafting table, and the work progressed quickly. He wanted to point out that teamwork *might* be a more efficient way to get by, but this was their world. And they weren't herding cattle.

Frida and Turner went ahead making armor and fashioning arrows together, not saying much, yet seeming to know what the other needed. When at last they ran out of feathers, they had to put off filling their slots with arrows.

"These ain't near enough," Turner said, closing his inventory. "We'll have to trade for some feathers as soon as we get to the village."

Frida crossed her fingers. "Hope we don't run into trouble on the way."

This reawakened Rob's worries. "I don't have anything to trade yet. Or anything to craft weapons from."

Turner placed a bow and a few arrows on top of one of the iron chest plates he'd made and shoved it over to Rob. "Here ya go, Newbie. You can pay me back with interest someday."

Rob glanced at him, thankful. The tattooed mercenary waved a hand emblazoned with a mountain biome, like the loan was no big deal. Then they each retreated to a corner, Frida blew out most of the torches, and they went to sleep for the night.

*

After a breakfast of apples, the three newly allied friends packed up their gear and stepped out into the leaf-filtered sunshine. But in no time, a jungle shower blew through.

As rain dripped through the dense tree canopy, Frida's brown leather cap kept her head dry. Turner donned a chainmail helmet that was nearly waterproof. Rob wished for the hat he'd lost at sea, but he wasn't about to complain. Besides, a jungle rainstorm was warm. And shade-loving orchids were blooming right before their eyes. It could've been worse.

"So, there's a village not far from here?" Rob asked, excited at the prospect of more humans and houses.

Maybe it *would* be more like his home. Maybe some-one would even know a way to get there.

"We'll be at the village by nightfall," Turner said, "unless something . . . interesting happens."

"Like what?"

Just as the question escaped Rob's lips, three dark forms with long limbs teleported up and over the group, landing behind them with a soft thud.

Rob turned to face them, but Frida blocked him. "Endermen! They got wet! They don't like that. Don't look at them!"

How was he supposed to not stare at a bunch of weird, black, gangly-legged creatures that were trying to surround them? Frida threw up a screen of the vines she'd cut the day before, and she and Turner crouched behind it, waving Rob over.

"You hold down the fort!" Turner whispered. "These ain't your friends!"

He drew his sword and burst from cover to attack the Endermen, which had already suffered rain dam-age. Turner killed all three in no time, and each dropped an Ender pearl as they ceased to be.

"Grab those, Newbie!" Turner directed. "Hang on to them until you find some more. You're the one who might need to locate an Ender portal."

Rob had no idea what Turner was talking about but thought the items might have trade value.

Frida reeled in her vine screen, and they walked on. To Rob's relief, the rain petered out and the canopy thinned above them. The darker it was, he knew, the greater the chance of something . . . *interesting* happening, as Turner had put it.

"There's a lake up ahead!" Frida called out. "Hey, Meat. Got a fishing pole? I'm getting hungry already."

"I can make one," Turner said. "Hang on!" He riffled through his inventory, dismantled a bow, and swiftly crafted a fishing rod.

Rob's mouth watered just thinking about a mess of trout, or catfish, or whatever kind of fish might live here. But as they approached the small lake, they could see that someone else had beat them to the spot.

A horse's whinny cut through the air, alerting a teenage boy sitting on the bank to their presence. The boy's skin was ultra pale, his brown, wavy hair cut close, and he was as thin as an Enderman, although not quite as long-limbed.

Rob felt the tension stretch like a live wire between his group and the teen.

"Catching anything?" Turner called casually.

The fellow nodded.

"What's biting today?" Frida asked.

As they arrived a few blocks away, the boy cried, "Pufferfish!" and hurled an object their way.

Frida ducked in one direction, and Turner ducked in the other. Rob's jaw had dropped, and he caught the spiny fish—in his mouth!

A wave of severe hunger hit him like a tsunami, and he thought he was going to be sick to his stomach. His arms and legs seized up, and he couldn't move. "I'm dying!" he yelled.

"It's just poison," Turner said, as though it were nothing.

"I've died scores of times," the fisherboy added. "You'll come back."

Frida turned to him angrily and growled, "We meant you no harm!"

He looked ashamed and tossed her a bottle of milk. "Here, patch him up. I always carry some with me when I'm fishing, just in case."

Frida held Rob's head up and helped him drink. He was amazed at how fast the effects of the poisonous pufferfish wore off.

From a thicket came another whinny, and the boy called to the horse that everything was okay.

"Where's your pony?" Rob asked, slurring his words a little, but desperately wanting to see a live animal again—one that didn't cause instant paralysis.

"That's Beckett, begging for sugar," the boy said, waving at the thatch of trees. "I tie him up while I fish;

otherwise, he wades in and scares everything off." He smiled apologetically at Rob. "I'm Jools. Sorry about the fish bomb. A guy can't be too careful around the biome boundaries."

"Mind if I try my luck?" Turner asked, pulling out his fishing rod.

"Be my guest," Jools said. "There's plenty more scaly types biting. I'm just hunting pufferfish for crafting potions."

"Good idea," Frida said. "I hear Dr. Dirt's army is still roaming the plains perimeter."

"Right-o. I want to be ready for them."

Something occurred to Rob. "If you've got a horse, can't you just outrun them?"

Jools grinned and shook his head. "Not on old Beckett. He's sound transportation, but a bit of a nag. Hence the need for potions."

Rob felt a kinship with another horseman, even one that had cast spells made from deadly fish. "I'm Rob. And this is Frida and Turner. We're on our way to the village to do some trading. I wish we could ride instead of walk."

"You can," Jools said. "I know where there's a whole herd of horses just waiting to be tamed. Unfortunately, it's on the other side of the boundary."

"I'd wrestle a skeleton any day for the chance to gentle a good horse," Rob said, then saw Turner roll his eyes. "Besides, horses might come in handy in the next fight." That got Turner's attention.

The mercenary pulled in a salmon and set his fishing rod down on the bank. Then he went over and peeked among the trees, and came back. "Hey, Jools. You say you know where to find a flock of these beasts?"

"A herd," Jools corrected. "They're not chickens."

"Might taste like chicken," Turner said, making Rob's stomach lurch again. "Just kidding. A quick getaway might be just what we need to make it to the village in one piece."

Rob cheered. "Now you're talking!"

Jools eyed his outfit. "I see you're wearing chaps. I'm mad about western garb. Do you ride?"

Rob puffed up beneath his vest. "Do I? I was the Far Western Sector Rodeo champion three years in a row. Got the belt buckle to prove it . . . at home. On my ranch," he added when Jools appeared skeptical.

"He's on the level," Frida said. "He's no griefer. This boy doesn't have a false bone in his body."

That made Rob feel good. He'd made a solid impression on her, and he could tell that Frida didn't trust many people.

"Well, seeing is believing," Jools said.

"I'll prove it to you," Rob replied. "Will you take us to the herd?"

"What'll you give me for doing it?"

Rob thought a moment. "How about some Ender pearls?"

The pale boy's eyes sparkled. "You've got a deal." He paused. "There's just one problem."

They waited.

"We've got to cross the border into the plains tonight. It's not safe to keep Beckett in the jungle when the mobs come out."

"I'm up for a fight!" declared Turner. He turned to Frida and Rob. "You guys in?"

Frida nodded fiercely.

It didn't seem to Rob like there was much choice. The sky was turning a soft purple, and night was coming on quickly. Besides, this might be the only chance to find some wild horses. He swallowed. "I'm in."

CHAPTER 4

AS THEY JOURNEYED ON, JOOLS WAS LESS THAN forthcoming about his background. Frida asked him about his spawn points, and he'd answered, "Here and there." When Turner inquired what Jools did for a living, he'd said, "Consultant." And when Rob asked about his riding skills, Jools claimed he was self-taught.

He seems like a nice enough guy, Rob thought. *But he could be a griefer. Or some kind of mercenary on the take, like Turner.* Rob held back all the questions he wanted to pose to the pale rider, who was now mounted on Beckett, a cream-colored stallion that was still several shades darker than the young man in the saddle. Rob turned his attention to the horse, which carefully moved forward at a slow march. He might not be the swiftest, but an animal that took care of its feet stayed healthy when other, more careless horses might damage their legs, sometimes fatally.

Still, Rob couldn't help breaking the silence. "I'd trust Beckett in a battle, Jools. He's sound, all right."

"He is that," Jools said proudly. Even the tight-lipped stranger gave way to flattery when it came to his pet.

"I'ma get me one of those," Turner announced, having the decency not to steal Beckett for himself. Not yet, anyway.

"You'll have to learn to ride," Frida reminded him.

Turner pointed at Jools. "He can do it. How hard can it be?"

Rob smiled to himself. It always looked like the horse was doing all the work.

As the sun sank and the sky darkened, the group settled into tense silence. Finally Jools halted Beckett, dismounted, and motioned for the others to gather around. "We'll find sentries not far from here," he informed them. "You might want to suit up."

Rob's gut tightened, and he put on the protective chest armor that Turner had given him.

"We can rendezvous at my camp," Jools offered. "It's just the other side of a dry wash."

Frida and Turner looked fierce in their chest plates and helmets. They pulled out their bows, and Rob did the same.

Frida squinted at Jools. "Where's your weaponry?" she asked, suspicion in her voice. A griefer wouldn't need to fend off Dr. Dirt's sentries.

Jools raised a flask. "Potion of invisibility!" He poured some down Beckett's gullet, and the horse gradually faded from view. Jools stepped into the invisible stirrup and heaved himself upward. "Sorry I haven't got enough for everyone." He downed the rest of the juice and whirled in the invisible saddle. "See you on the other side!" he called, and with a cluck and a whinny, the pair was gone.

Turner nudged Frida with a tattooed elbow. "D'you think he's on the level?"

She thought a moment. "I'd give him fifty-fifty," she said, and Rob silently agreed. Clearly, she was a good judge of character.

They set off again in the direction of the boundary. Rob couldn't help but feel as though he were approaching a cliff. He wished he had a potion or two in his inventory . . . but this time, he'd have to rely on his wits.

Suddenly, he heard a *thoop!* An arrow landed inches from his foot. Seeing it stuck in the ground like a party toothpick, it seemed so harmless.

The next one, which glanced off his chest armor, however, seemed much less innocent.

"Ambush!" he yelled.

The sound of rattling bones filled the air. In the murky light, Rob could see a half-dozen skeletons approach, their bows drawn and then refilled with arrows as fast as they could let them fly.

The three armored friends avoided hits as they returned fire, Frida and Turner knocking out two attackers apiece while Rob struggled to get the hang of archery. When the remaining two mobsters bore down on him, they loosed twice as many arrows as it seemed possible to shoot, but their aim was no good. From the corner of his eye, Rob saw that Frida and Turner were reloading. These two monsters were his, and his alone!

The enemies' closeness was in his favor. He sighted and drew back his bowstring. *Thwang!* His single arrow impaled the first skeleton, went on through, and took out the second.

His eyes widened. "Did you see that?" he called to his friends.

But his victory was soon forgotten.

With a rumba of rattling bones, a second wave of skeletons came charging from fifteen blocks away. Behind them came a gravelly shout: "Turn back or surrender! This boundary belongs to Dr. Dirt!"

Rob quaked, wishing he were mounted and could gallop away, out of range. But Frida grimaced and yelled back, "Boundaries belong to no man! Identify yourself!"

"I am Lady Craven, second-in-command, Griefers Imperial Army!" The reply sounded as though the syllables had been spit from a cement mixer.

Frida set an arrow and moved her bow in the direction of the voice as Turner and Rob prepared to meet the onslaught.

"Second? Ha! Dr. Dirt does not dare to show his face on these lines?"

"He has bigger fish to fry, minnow," Lady Craven replied. "And he has me to swallow the rest of you!"

Rob's eyes left the approaching skeletons for a moment to watch Frida. She was intent, sweeping her bow, seeming to track the sound of Lady Craven. When Frida fixed her target, she yelled, "Die!" and released the bowstring.

Rob held his breath.

Turner hesitated.

Even the attacking skeletons paused to see whether Frida's arrow would hit its distant target.

There was no sound.

Then a diabolical laugh filled the air. "Your puny sticks and stones cannot harm me. My wings are like a shield of iron. I cannot die!"

The skeletons resumed their attack, rushing now at the three defenders, both sides bent on claiming ground. Rob filled and refilled his bow, picking off monsters one by one, but still there were more.

Then there was a *boom,* and a sound like a gong
rang out, masking the bone rattling and bone breaking, and ringing in Rob's ears. An explosion lit the
sky. Rob and the others froze. Would the next blast
come their way? Instead, a raspy shriek sailed across
the darkened field, followed by the sudden retreat of
the remaining skeletons.

When, at last, quiet fell, Frida, Turner, and Rob
dared to move again. Rob patted his body to make
sure all his parts were still there. Frida and Turner
leapfrogged ahead, picking up the bones and arrows
that the dying skeletons had dropped.

"What the heck was that?" Rob asked.

"It was me. A friendly," a human voice responded.
"Don't shoot!"

*

Out of the shadows strolled a buff female with skin
the color of stormy skies, backlit by the glow from
trees that burned in the aftermath of the blast. She
was more curves than angles and barely covered by
black, short shorts and a crop top. Her long, black,
curly hair was pulled back in a ponytail. Rob's heart
jumped. If a girl could be his hero, she was it. More
substantial than Frida, possibly stronger than Turner,
and definitely more tan than Jools, this young woman

appeared to hold the world in her hands. She had just run off an entire platoon of skeletons and their griefer commander, after all.

"You saved our ham bones, stranger," Turner admitted.

"H-how can we thank you?" Rob stuttered.

Frida scowled. "Not so fast. Who are you? How do we know you're not one of them?" she demanded, backing off as the woman advanced.

"I'm Stormie—the original one, not that imposter who says she's been to the world boundary but has really only gone as far as the extreme hills."

The hair stood up against Rob's neck. "Extreme hills? You've been there?"

"Which time?" Stormie asked.

Turner grunted. "I've heard of you. Folks in the cold taiga said you tamed a wolf without a bone. How'd you do that?"

She clucked at him. "Now, now," she said, patting Turner's desert biome tattoo on his biceps. "Let's not be greedy. A gal's got to have her secrets."

"I've heard of you, too," Frida said, then grinned. "Most of it I didn't really believe."

Stormie gave her arm a squeeze. "That, I do believe. How's *this* for a dose of reality?" She drew an object from her satchel and tossed it at Frida, who caught it in one hand.

Frida opened her fingers and examined the thing, and a knowing smile spread across her green face. "Girlfriend!" she exclaimed.

Turner muscled up to her. "Let me see." He gaped. "Yowza!"

It had been a long . . . interesting day, and Rob was tired, and just a little bit annoyed. "Would somebody please tell me what's going on?" he snapped.

His tone broke through Frida's reverie. "Sorry," she apologized, dangling a golden chain before his eyes. It was a pendant sporting a gem-encrusted charm made of two golden Ds fused together. "It's Dr. Dirt's signature," she explained, handing it back to the woman.

"All his lackeys wear them," Stormie explained. "So, why are y'all fighting one of Dirt's squadrons?"

"We're just crossing into the plains on some business," Frida told her. "I've been tangling with smaller skeleton sentries at every biome crossing for a while now, but this mob was nasty. You?"

"Same deal." Stormie sat down on the ground cross-legged. "I'm beat. Believe me, I've crossed a lot of boundaries in the last string of days."

"We appreciate the boost," Turner said, joining her on the ground. "What did you do to Lady Craven?"

"She was wearing those ridiculous iron wings, thinking she was invincible and all that. I rang her chimes with a TNT cannon."

"Nice tune," Turner said.

Frida resumed gathering the items dropped by the skeletons, stacking them in her inventory. Rob just stood there, staring at Stormie in awe.

"Who's this sweet pea?" she asked Turner, who grunted again.

Frida joined them and introductions were made. But after a short rest they all got to their feet again.

"We'd better head for the rendezvous point," Frida said. "A friend of ours is waiting there at shelter. You're welcome to come along."

"Solid. Normally I'd have somewhere to be, but tonight I could use a break."

They moved off in the direction of the army's retreat, their way lit by the still-burning brush in the distance.

"Do you think they're gone for good?" Rob asked.

"*Good* is relative," Stormie replied. "Any reprieve is good, but Dirt's got uglies stationed from here to kingdom come."

"We're afraid they're sweeping across the entire Overworld," Frida added.

"Wouldn't doubt it," Stormie said. "I've run into them at every single boundary I've crossed in recent memory."

"What do you think they're up to?" Frida asked.

"No good. At this point, it would take a whole army to bring them down, I'm afraid."

Rob doubted that this Amazon was ever afraid. But what she'd said had given him an idea. "That's the type of army I'd like to lead someday," he said aloud.

Turner laughed, and Frida cut him a look.

"That's a selfless ambition, Rob," Stormie said. "Maybe you'd make a good commander."

This embarrassed the cowboy, who had never commanded anything but a herd of cattle. "Well, I . . ."

As the others discussed the impossibility of such a task, Rob couldn't help thinking that if anyone could stand up to the evil griefers, it was this group: Frida was stealthy, resourceful, and discerning. Turner was strong, brave, and a real jerk—something that worked well on the offensive, for sure. And Stormie . . . well she was the type of soldier a commander could only dream about.

But such an independent bunch would never listen to a peace-loving range rider like him. Would they?

*

The four picked their way through the smoldering battlefield and arrived at the dry wash without further incident. From there, they could see Jools's campfire and hear Beckett nicker a greeting. They crossed the shallow gully and called out to Jools, so he wouldn't be alarmed and start pelting them with splash potions.

Jools also had heard stories about their new ally.

"Left your undies as a banner at the world boundary, did you? Or was that the other Stormie?"

"That was me!" she snapped. "Blast that girl, trying to ride my coattails . . . er, underwear tails. . . ." She smiled sweetly at Jools. "What's your claim to fame, bro?"

Stormie's charisma broke through his wall of ice. "I'm a detail consultant," he told her. "Some people get the big picture. I cut it into little pieces and analyze it. Worth a fortune to the right employer."

"Yeah, well, ya can't kill a mess of zombies with a detail," Turner grumbled. "Where were you when Lady Craven's skelemob tore into us?"

Jools sat back, unperturbed. "Right here. Thinking my brains out. That's kept my head attached to my neck all this time."

"Jools used a potion of invisibility to move him and his horse to safe camp," Rob explained to Stormie. "That was pretty smart."

"Yeah, well, *smart* won't—"

Jools raised his hands. "I know, I know, Turner. *Smart* won't kill an army of whatever." He reached over toward the fire and drew out some chicken legs, which he passed around the group. "Killing monsters is not my thing," Jools continued. "Figuring out *how* to kill them is."

Stormie raised an eyebrow. "A strategist. We don't have one of those. Could be valuable in a war."

Jools grinned. "It's nice to be appreciated."

CHAPTER 5

HAVING FULL ARSENALS OF ARROWS WAS AS soothing to the band of travelers as glasses of warm milk. With the distant trees burning like torches and the broad plains open around them, the group felt safe from other mob attacks and slept well that night.

Rob woke first. He rose from his wool bedroll, feeling almost normal. As sunshine perforated the pink clouds, he could hear the soft munch of a horse grazing nearby. It was just like old times. Present company excluded, of course.

Frida lay on her back near the cold campfire, snoring lightly. Jools slumped not far from her under a lean-to made of sunflowers. Turner was curled in the fetal position, clutching his helmet like a teddy bear. And Stormie . . .

. . . was awake. She caught Rob staring at her and winked.

"What's the plan today, Captain?" she asked, rising.

Rob's skin darkened several shades of red. "We're off to round up some horses and trade with the villagers. I'm not sure which comes first."

"Just take charge." She waved at the others sleeping. "They'll fall in line."

"If I have my way, it's broncs first, townsfolk second."

"Horses it is, then!"

"You're coming with us?"

She nodded.

Rob couldn't believe his luck. He had no doubt that Stormie would be a good hand in a roundup. *Competent* seemed to be her last name.

The others began to stir. Casting a glance at Stormie, Rob began barking out orders. "Frida. Check the campfire for usable coals. Jools, make sure Beckett isn't hungry. He's going to be our scout. And Turner, quit hugging that helmet and pack up. It's time to go!"

"Who died and left him boss?" muttered the mercenary, sitting up and jamming his helmet back on his head as the others set to work.

"Guys," Rob said, "when it comes to horses, I'm your man."

Turner yawned and lay back down. "I'm thinking maybe we hit the village first for some R and R."

Rob nudged him with a toe. "This isn't some wild goose chase. Getting horses could save your skin."

"I do all right on my own."

"That's funny. Yesterday you were all for the plan when you knew the mobs were coming out." Rob gathered up his bedroll. "From what I saw during the battle, a mounted group working together could have really kicked some grass."

"You mean, a cavalry?" asked Stormie.

"Yep. Advancing. Retreating. Riding in formation. Your weapons will be lots more effective from horseback." Jools, Frida, and Turner were all paying attention now. "I've done a lot of reading on the subject. Even practiced some of the moves. It's kind of a hobby of mine."

"Like, battle reenactments?" Turner said, even more interested.

"Yeah. I never thought I'd actually be *in* a battle, though."

"I second the motion," Jools said. "I'm not much for putting myself in harm's way, but I could be your man at the war table," he offered.

"Think you boys could teach me to ride?" Frida asked. "I've always wanted to try."

"Sure thing," Rob replied. "Ever been on a horse, you two?" he asked Stormie and Turner. They shook their heads.

"That don't matter," Turner assured him. "I can fight off of anything."

"Same here," Stormie said.

Rob envied their confidence. "Well, let's not put the cart before the horse. We've got to get mounted first."

*

Jools and Beckett led the foot soldiers across the plains toward where the strategist had sighted the wild herd. "The other horses are less likely to run off if they see Beckett up front," Rob explained to the group.

To pass the time, Stormie entertained everyone with stories of her adventures. It seemed as though she'd visited every corner of the world, and—if she were telling the truth—met every villain and lived to tell the tale.

"I don't get it," Turner said, perplexed. "How do ya make a living off of gallivanting around playing pick-up-sticks all the time?"

Frida elbowed him. "It's not always about the money, Meat. Some people have a thirst for life."

"*And* a thirst for cash," Stormie confessed. "I track what I see. Mineral deposits. Good farmland. Terrain best avoided."

"Anyone paying attention sees that stuff," Turner argued. "Who'd trade good emeralds for a bubble of common knowledge?"

Stormie pulled a flat parchment out of her inventory. "It's called a map, Meat. And it's worth a lot of scratch."

Jools brought Beckett to a halt, and they all crowded around her to see the map she'd crafted.

Frida wrinkled her green brow. "Now *that* looks useful. See this *X*, Turner? That means *You are here.*"

He scowled. "I know how maps work." He flicked the page with his thumb and forefinger. "And you don't get to call me Meat," he said, glaring at Stormie.

"Okay, Meat."

Turner stomped off. The gang returned to the trail.

Along the way, Frida used a pair of shears she'd brought to cut grass. Every now and then she'd give a happy, little cry and collect some seeds, which she stored in her inventory. "If we're going to have a string of horses, we're going to need something to feed them, wherever we go."

"Good thinking," Rob said.

They stopped at a watering hole to give Beckett a drink. Sure enough, the palomino horse waded all the way in, soaking his rider up to his chest. Jools just laughed. Prickly though he was with people, the guy loved his horse.

As Beckett splashed about, the group heard a rumbling, which grew louder and louder.

"Thunder?" Frida guessed.

Stormie checked the sky. "Without any rain or lightning?"

Just then, a passive animal mob raced toward the group, manes and tails streaming in the wind. Beckett called out to them with his highest-pitched whinny. He must have said the right thing, because the herd approached at a gallop and skidded to a stop at the edge of the watering hole.

The mob milled around a minute, until a black horse separated itself, walked into the water first, and took a drink. The rest followed, slurping their fill while the black horse stood guard.

"That's the one I want," Turner whispered.

"He's the boss," Rob said. "The others will act on his lead."

"Then that's the one we want to tame first," Jools pointed out. He took some planks and sticks from his inventory and crafted a series of fences, which he fashioned into a corral. He handed Stormie a stick and had her stand at the opening to make a gate once they had lured a horse inside.

"Me first!" Turner insisted.

The wild herd had finished with the water and stood next to the pond, grazing. Turner walked up to the black horse, and without so much as an introduction, sprang onto its back. He grabbed a hunk of black mane and said, "Giddyup!"

A half second later, he was staring up at his friends from the ground, waiting for his vision to clear. "What the—?"

Jools smirked. "Perhaps you'd best try that one, Rob."

Rob had been sizing up the herd boss, a black stallion with a white star on its forehead and white socks on its hind legs. It reminded him of his trusty horse, Pistol, back home: smart, confident, and not about to take orders from a lesser being.

"Anybody got any sugar?" Rob asked.

"Always." Jools tossed him a piece.

Rob took the sugar inside the corral and sat down on the ground, his back to the black horse. He began to hum tunelessly under his breath.

Turner folded his arms, certain that the cowboy was giving up before he'd even begun. Frida and Jools, though, sensed what he was up to and gravitated toward the fence, settling themselves on a cross rail to watch. Stormie held the "gate" at the ready.

At first, the black horse paid them no mind, continuing to graze or nip at one of the other beasts when it got too close to his eating spot. As Rob rolled the block of sugar around in his hand, though, he caught the horse's attention. Little by little, the distance between them narrowed as the black horse sidled toward the corral, then through the opening, then up to Rob's back.

At last, Rob could feel him breathing down his neck. "Now!" he cried, and Stormie slid the gate shut.

The horse quickly assessed his new situation, eyeing the fence and the sugar in Rob's hand. Making up his mind, he ducked for Rob, snatched the sugar, and dashed for the fence, jumping it handily. The stallion rejoined his herd and went back to grazing as if nothing had happened.

Groans rose from the group outside the fence. Turner scratched his head and said, "This is more complicated than I thought."

Rob didn't move, though. He, too, acted as though nothing unusual had taken place. He continued humming and pretended to roll a nonexistent sugar block around in his hand.

Pretty soon the black horse raised its head to observe the cowboy in the pen. The horse warred with his curiosity, then finally, to everyone's surprise, he got a running start and jumped back inside the corral to confront the stranger.

Rob held out a flat hand to show him it held nothing. In the next instant, he was on the horse's back.

Everyone held their breath, waiting for the explosion.

Rob gave a cluck and squeezed the horse's sides, and it walked out toward the fence line, nice as pie.

"Brilliant!" called Jools. "That almost never happens."

It happens to me, Rob thought, pantomiming a doff of a hat. Even without the sombrero, he was still a heck of a cowboy.

*

The rest of the session didn't go as well. They managed to lure three more horses into the pen using the black stallion, whom Rob had named Saber, as a decoy. But taming them was not so easy. They were out of sugar, and the two mares and young colt they'd chosen were not interested in being ridden without payment of some kind.

Stormie got dumped by a chocolate-brown mare three times in a row. Turner tried to ride one horse after the other, getting dumped soundly by each one. Frida nearly got kicked and never managed to get on at all. Rob sat atop Saber, making helpful suggestions, and Jools called out advice from Beckett's saddle, but they were of no help. Still, this wasn't the group to throw in the towel, no matter how much of a bath they were taking.

"What I need is a saddle," Turner said, splayed out on the hard ground after his third try. "Something with one a those knobs on it to hang on to."

"But we're in the middle of nowhere. How are we going to find a saddle?" Rob asked.

"Could fish for one," Jools suggested. "But that's kind of hit or miss."

"I've got one," came an unfamiliar voice.

Rob, Turner, Jools, Frida, and Stormie all gasped, shocked that someone had been able to approach them without their knowledge. Beckett hadn't whinnied. Saber hadn't even switched his tail.

Peeking over the top rail of the corral was a slip of a girl with pink skin, shiny black hair, and one gold earring.

"Who're you?" Turner demanded.

"And what are you doing with a saddle?" Frida added, seeing no horse accompanying the girl.

"I'm Kim." She smiled. "How can I help you?"

Jools peered down at her from his perch astride Beckett. "I doubt that you can help us. Even with a saddle." He waved a hand as though chasing a fly.

"Trying to gentle 'em? Let me try."

Without waiting for an invitation, she scrambled over the rail and into the enclosure. She chirruped, and the bay colt and bay mare with the same markings walked right up to her. With a leap, she vaulted onto them both, standing upright with one leg on the back of each horse. The next thing the group knew, she was cantering them around in a circle as though it were the center ring of a three-ring circus.

Finally, after encouraging her mounts to pirouette side by side in a loop, she threw her arms out in front of her and performed an alley-oop onto the ground.

Jools slowly applauded. Frida, Stormie, and Rob joined in, cheering.

"How'd she do that?" Turner muttered, crossing his decorated arms.

"Yeah, where'd you learn to ride like that?" Rob asked the new girl.

"I learned by watching," she replied. Then she walked over and opened the corral gate, and the three loose horses bolted out, back to the herd.

"What'd you do that for?" Turner yelled. "It took us half a day to get them in here."

Kim turned to him with a wry smile. "They'll come back." She paused. "They're mine."

*

It turned out that the bronc whisperer, as they were now calling Kim, was a horse breeder. "I have a place not too far from here," she said. "I've got an extra saddle there you can use—or trade for. In fact, I've got three horses that are already tame and set to ride."

"Name your price," said Stormie, obviously impressed.

"Well, I've got plenty of emeralds already," Kim said, thinking. "What I could really use is some help with the haying."

"You mean, like, work?" Turner translated.

"Physical labor?" Jools wrinkled his nose. "I've got my own horse."

"You can always use another. I've got some racing types available." Kim was a good salesperson.

"I like them slow," Jools said, patting Beckett's neck.

"I don't," Turner blurted out. "Let's go eyeball 'em."

The other two women looked at Rob.

"Let's," he agreed. "I'm sure that Kim here has something suitable for the two of you." He and Jools dismounted and led their horses to give them a rest. "Guess I'll have to find something to trade for Saber."

"No worries," Kim told him. "I was never able to get close enough to tame that one. He's yours fair and square."

They all set out for Kim's ranch, Rob feeling on top of the world.

Kim walked in between Stormie and Frida. "Why are you shopping for mounts if you don't mind my asking? You don't seem like horsey types."

"You guessed right," Frida said. "We're not out for a pleasure ride."

Stormie motioned at Rob. "Our homeboy Rob, here, is going to help us form a cavalry. We've got to take care of some business."

Kim looked at her. "Zombie business?"

"Wrong. We've got a date with Dr. Dirt, if we ever want to travel freely again in the Overworld. He's the one we need to take out."

Kim nodded. "I've heard his armies are crisscrossing the map. That's why I pretty much stay here on the plains. I've got most everything I need. I grow my own wheat, hay, and vegetables, and I can trade in the village for most everything else."

Turner had come up alongside her. "You say, *most*. What is it you're missing?"

The pink-skinned girl hesitated. "I'm . . . not sure. It's just, every now and then, I feel like there must be something out there for me, over the horizon."

Rob sensed a kindred spirit. "I know what you mean," he said. "Myself, I'm bound for the extreme hills. Not that I've ever been there. But that's a long story."

"We've got time," Kim said.

So they filled her in on Rob's plight and the danger that he and the others had already faced in beginning their journey. Stormie had agreed to accompany them as a guide since she had maps and knew the terrain.

But they all realized that Dr. Dirt's stronghold had to be broken before they could boundary hop with any safety.

Kim stayed quiet as they replayed the details. When her spread came into view, about fifty blocks away, she looked over her shoulder at Rob. "Can I ask you a question? Would it be all right if I joined your company?"

"Sure—it's not my company," he stammered, "but you're welcome to ride with us. We can always use a good hand. But how come?"

"What do you mean, how come?" She acted like the answer was obvious. "Why, to save the world, dummy."

CHAPTER 6

ROB FELT LIKE A KID IN A CANDY STORE AT THE horse farm, where mares, stallions, colts, and fillies of all colors and sizes ambled, cavorted, and pushed up to the fence to greet the visitors. Kim knew the horses' personalities and abilities. Rob knew those of his friends. Together they played matchmaker, eventually pairing Frida, Stormie, and Turner with suitable mounts.

Then it was time for their first riding lesson. Kim produced a saddle and showed Turner how to tack up. She told Stormie and Frida, "You two can trade for more saddles in the village, and Rob, too, if he needs one. Meanwhile, you look steady enough to handle bareback riding if we don't go any faster than a trot."

Kim helped them get mounted, instructing them to put their arms out at their sides to find their centers of balance. Stormie sat atop a black and white paint horse, while Frida had been matched with a shiny black pony with a spotted rump. Turner squirmed in the saddle on the coarse, gray stallion that Kim had picked out for him, a blocky quarter horse that had more chest and barrel than all the other horses put together.

"Nothing to hold on to here," Turner complained of his hornless saddle.

"We won't be working cattle," Rob said. "Besides, how do you think you'd shoot arrows off of old Duff here if you were hanging onto something else?"

"In fact," Kim said, "I want you all to start out riding no-handed. Learn to steer with your legs."

"Where's your mount?" asked Jools, who was standing near Beckett, feeding him bits of apple, which Kim had provided.

"Oh, I don't ride," she said. "I mostly teleport where I need to go. I was just keeping you guys company on the walk over."

Interesting, Rob thought. Staying on the ground— or hovering slightly above it—gave Kim more opportunity to study each horse's behavior. *She really knows them.*

The gang spent some time getting a feel for their horses at a walk and then a trot. Turner was surprised to stay upright as Duff picked up his feet and passed the others.

"He's fast, but he's smooth," Kim mentioned. She made similar comments about Armor and Ocelot, the paint and the pony that the girls were riding. Armor was the braver of the two, but Ocelot could maneuver like a . . . well, like an ocelot. And they already knew that Saber was an ace jumper.

Rob liked the mix of talents in this mob, kind of like the skills that each of their human counterparts brought to the table. Working together, he thought, they'd be a pretty formidable team.

"Good going, gang," Kim said. "Now, if you'll just put your horses up, you can come help me bale hay and consider yourselves paid in full."

Even Turner couldn't argue with settling the debt that was already paying off for him. He'd figured out that by rubbing Duff's shoulder in a certain spot the horse would respond in kind with a nice back scratch. "We're gonna get along just fine, pal," he said, patting Duff's side.

The sun crossed the sky's midpoint as the group finished forming the last hay block and stacked it in Kim's big barn. Rob noted that she'd crafted all of the outbuildings quite sturdily and had even found time to add nice touches like flower pots and emerald inlay. If he weren't bent on getting home to his own ranch, he wouldn't mind staying here, maybe forever.

But duty called.

"We'd best get to town," he said.

Kim was satisfied with everyone's ability to sit their horses, so they remounted and walked across the plains toward the village. Kim hopped in slow motion, teleporting behind or ahead of them. The horses appeared to be used to this movement and paid her no mind.

The gang soon reached the stone walls of the village, which were unguarded, and passed under a large arch. Lining the main street was a neat collection of tidy shops and houses. Villagers stopped to watch the strangers march by. Kim appeared to be quite popular. "Friends of yours?" asked a melon hawker as she teleported past. "Nice to see you!" called an older woman who was scrubbing a cobblestone walkway. Even the patrolling iron golem sent her a salute. Kim nodded and waved.

They pulled up in front of the butcher shop and tied their horses. "We'll meet back here," Kim said, and the women headed for the leather worker's shop, while the men went to visit the blacksmith.

Inside the smithy the heat of the forge nearly pushed Jools, Turner, and Rob back out the door. A sturdy-looking woman with red skin greeted them with a hammer in one hand and a horseshoe in the other. "I'm Sundra," she said. "Make yourselves at home. Be with you in a minute." She finished shoeing a mule that stood in one corner, its chestnut coat shining in the glow of the furnace.

"Now, what can I do you for?" she asked.

"I'd like some obsidian," Jools said.

"I'm in the market for an iron sword and a helmet," Rob said, figuring the latter was the next best thing to a cowboy hat.

Turner stuck a finger through his chainmail helmet. "Got a hole here that needs fixing," he said.

Sundra accommodated their requests, and they plied her with emeralds. Rob had acquired a handful from Kim, who'd paid him for his help with the haying since he didn't owe her anything for the use of Saber.

Sundra smiled, showing a row of gold teeth. "So, what're you three hunks of burnin' love doing in the village?"

Jools and Rob coughed. Turner preened, answering, "Truth be told, we're on a fact-finding mission."

"You haven't heard anything about Dr. Dirt's mobs being on the march around here, have you?" Rob asked.

"Heard? Seen," Sundra corrected him. "We've had to employ a night watch on the perimeter. Our iron golem was just manning the gate, but Dirt's skeletons used ladders to scale the walls one night. Took out three villagers and a pig."

"You don't say," Turner murmured.

"So, he's venturing beyond the biome boundaries," Jools noted. "He's getting bolder."

Rob placed his new iron helmet on his head. "So are we."

*

Jools and Rob finished their trading and wanted to explore the village.

"I'll just hang back here," Turner said, jabbing a thumb toward the forge. "Might learn something useful." Sundra batted her eyes as he leaned over the counter conspiratorially.

His partners shrugged at each other and stepped back outside into the sunshine.

Meanwhile, Kim had led the other women to the leather worker's studio. "Aswan is a master with leather," she said. "Not to mention, a bit of a black marketeer. Anything you can't find elsewhere, he'll have it. Or know someone who does."

"Kim, my devotion!" the white-aproned craftsman called out, greeting the bronc whisperer.

"Aswan, these are my friends Stormie and Frida."

He appraised them admiringly. "If I weren't already in love with you, my flower, you'd have some competition."

Stormie and Frida jostled each other, obviously pleased.

"Is this a social call?" Aswan asked hopefully.

"We're here on business," Kim said, nodding at Stormie. "She'd like some leather boots. And Frida needs some leggings."

Aswan was clearly disappointed, but he was a professional. "Let me measure you, girls."

As he was enjoying the perks of his job, Kim told him that their group had purchased a few horses from her and needed three saddles.

"I've got some top-of-the-line ones," he said, "but they're pricey. Ten emeralds apiece." He put down his measuring tape and wrote down some figures.

Stormie reached into her satchel and produced the gemstone pendant that Lady Craven had dropped. "How about *this* for the whole lot?" she said.

Frida shot her a glance. "You're trading with that?"

"There's more where that came from," Stormie said.

Aswan's eyes sparkled. He wiped his hands on his apron and reached for the pendant.

"Not so fast!" Stormie pulled the necklace out of reach. "We need one more item if you want this as payment."

Aswan narrowed his eyes. "And what would that be?"

"Information," Stormie answered, knowing that any good village leather worker would be up on the local gossip.

"I think we can trade for that," Aswan said with a knowing smile, taking the pendant from her.

Aswan invited the three women into the back of his studio, where the cutting and sewing took place. As he worked on their protective clothing, he told them what he had learned about Dr. Dirt's recent movements.

"I keep my ears open, and I know a lot of folks," he said. "Every single trader that's come through from outside the plains has tussled with one or another of Dirt's mobs. Jungle, forest, taiga boundaries," he ticked off on his fingers. "Mountains, ocean . . ." He ran out of fingers. "He's spreading his ranks like the plague."

Once outside with their purchases, Kim turned to Stormie. "None of that sounded good, did it?"

"Any intel is good intel," she countered. "We're going to need a place to train, somewhere that's at least semi-safe and defendable." She pulled out her map and they gathered around to survey it.

"We should go where there's plenty of room and fodder for the horses," Kim said.

Frida pointed at a spot. "Are you thinking what I'm thinking?"

"Bryce Mesa!" they all said at once.

"The mesa's isolated enough to be overlooked—" Stormie began.

"—but fortified all around," Frida finished. "It sits in this natural bowl of rock."

"And there's water for the horses," Kim added, pointing out a blue zigzag. "And pockets of good, red sand. Jools will be happy. Red sand is great for growing sugarcane, so he can satisfy Beckett's sweet tooth."

Frida frowned. "My grass seed won't take in that sand or hard clay, though."

"Don't worry," Stormie said. "We can haul in grass from the savanna on the north side." She held up two palms, and Kim slapped them. "Let's go tell the boys!"

*

They all met at the butcher shop, where they stocked their inventories with cooked pork chops and chicken strips, intending to brine them and dry them in the sun so they'd keep for the time being. Rob picked up some new cowboy boots, custom-made by Aswan. Then they stopped in at the library, where Kim traded some emeralds for a compass to help them navigate unfamiliar lands.

They all agreed that Bryce would be the ideal hideout where they could hone their cavalry skills before taking on Dr. Dirt's army. Its southern boundary adjoined the extreme hills, Rob's ultimate destination.

"Too bad it's so far out from the village, though," Turner regretted. "I wouldn't mind seeing more of Sundra."

Jools called to mind the burly blacksmith. "She's what you call . . . durable," he said.

"I think it's love," Rob teased.

"Makes for cheap trade!" Turner flashed the chain-mail leggings he'd wangled from her. "They match my helmet."

"Real sentimental chap," Jools observed.

Frida was not impressed. "Look, we'd better hit the trail. Sun's sinking."

The sky had reddened to the west, and they would have to make good time to build shelter on the trail before darkness. Soon after remounting and filing out the village gate, though, they saw a cloud of dust headed their way from the plains.

"What is that?" Rob said. Saber sensed Rob's concern and raised his head, trying to figure out who—or what—was approaching. "Kim, climb aboard." The cowboy pulled Kim up behind his new saddle, just to be safe.

"Griefers!" came a cry from atop the village wall. "And their mob! Shut the gate!"

The six friends looked at one another, realizing they were about to be locked out in the open to face the oncoming trouble. Rob wheeled Saber around and yelled, "Let's make a run for it. . . . Hang on, Turner!" Saber galloped back toward the wall, and the rest of the horses followed. Rob needn't have worried, though. As they retreated through the gate, Turner's horse, Duff, took the lead, rebalancing his unsettled rider so he wouldn't tumble off and land underfoot.

"Take a left and head for Aswan's!" Kim directed. "He's got a stone shelter big enough for the horses."

It wouldn't do for griefers to know about the horses any sooner than was necessary. They were the gang's edge, an advantage soon to become its own weapon.

Aswan saw them coming and waved them into his sanctuary—already lit by torches.

"Expecting visitors?" Kim asked him pointedly.

"Right about this time every night," he replied.

Turner yelped, "We're just gonna *hide*?"

"Lay low," Kim corrected.

"Sound advice," Jools agreed.

"Not in my book!" Turner made for the door on foot.

Frida watched him pull his sword, and then she glanced at Rob. No way could she leave Turner to go it alone. "I've got his back," she said, and ran after him.

Aswan swung the iron door shut behind her, and they all settled in the bunker, waiting for the worst.

A roar of thunder rose, nearly drowning out the clacking of bones and the *ping* of arrows bouncing off the village gate. Periodically, they could hear a villager shriek and a thud as he or she fell from the parapet.

"This is awful!" Rob groaned. "Isn't there something we can do to help them?"

"There is." Stormie set her chin. "Live to fight another day."

Rob knew she was right. They were unprepared, and their ranks had been split. He couldn't help but worry for Turner and Frida. They were some of the toughest fighters he knew, but they were outnumbered.

"They'll be all right," Kim murmured, reading Rob's mind.

After what seemed like an eon, but was probably only a few short minutes, they heard banging on Aswan's door.

"Open up!" came Turner's gruff voice.

Aswan eyed Kim, who nodded. He cracked open the door, and Turner pushed Frida into the structure ahead of him. They collapsed to the floor, panting, as Aswan sealed them all in safely.

"What's going on out there?" Stormie demanded.

"Griefers," gasped Turner.

Frida got to her hands and knees. "Griefers on skeleton horses!"

The group received this news with horror.

"Them things're hard to kill," Turner puffed.

Frida recovered her breath. "All you'll get is one clear shot. But at least skelehorses can't be armored."

"But I thought they stuck to the biome boundaries. Why are they attacking the village?" Kim asked.

Just then, an amplified voice rang through the streets, high-pitched and deliberate.

"People . . . of . . . this . . . village! I, Dr. Dirt, claim your resources . . . for my army. Toss everything out through the gate, and I might not burn you all alive!"

"He's not getting my inventory," Turner vowed.

"Ssh!" Stormie put a hand on his shoulder. "He doesn't know we're here."

Misery washed over Rob as they heard the clanging and thudding of hurled goods that the villagers had no choice but to surrender. Aswan wisely sat silently by his guests, but showed signs of distress as he hid while his countrymen suffered.

When, at last, the clatter abated and they heard the town gate slam shut once more, Aswan pushed his door ajar and peeked outside.

Now they could hear even more clearly the high-pitched calls that filled the night: "You . . . have . . . complied, villagers. As . . . you . . . must!" Then they heard a volley of arrows hit the streets and a crackling sound in their wake. Dr. Dirt's cruel laughter shot out like fireworks. "I . . . shall . . . burn you anyway . . . sorry, losers!"

The glow that followed was no harmless light show. Every wooden structure within the village walls had been set ablaze!

Now the six friends and their host poured from the stone enclosure, leaving the horses milling safely inside. Even Jools lent a hand. They joined in with the villagers to battle the fire, punching blocks, smothering them, and forming a human bucket brigade to douse the flames. Men and women shouted and ran to save their few remaining belongings. Smoke filled the streets. Little by little, the fire was contained, then extinguished.

The survivors roamed about in a daze, picking up debris and asking folks if they were all right. A pile of iron ingots and dead poppies indicated that the town's iron golem had been neutralized at the gate.

"You'd better stay here for the night," Aswan suggested, with only a hint of flirtation. Kim gratefully accepted for the group.

As they sat on the floor among their horses, Rob tried to find a silver lining to their situation. "There couldn't be a better time to form a cavalry unit," he said, and Stormie nodded.

Turner growled, "If you must know, I'm having second thoughts. Skeleton jockeys are way out of my league."

Frida furrowed her brow. "It does up the ante, doesn't it?"

Jools wiped his soot-darkened face with a fist. "Maybe we should quit while we're ahead. . . ."

"Snap out of it, you wussies!" Kim scolded. "Skeleton horses or no, they're still horses. With the right strategy, we can handle them. Maybe even harness their power."

"Humph!" Turner remained unconvinced.

"I've got Beckett to think of. . . ." Jools said, moving over to his horse and stroking his neck.

"Guys!" Stormie got up to stand behind Rob. "I'm sure our captain will find a way to overcome their ranks."

Rob appreciated her confidence in him, but even he was near despair. *Griefers on skeleton horses? Villages burning, boundaries taken . . .* He had read nothing about all this in the old cavalry manuals he'd studied. They would need more than his know-how to bring down Dr. Dirt. If only Rob had a mentor. Someone who had been through something similar.

"Jools," Kim said quietly. "In your line of work, you must have come across somebody who survived the First War. . . . Haven't you?"

At one time, when the Overworld was young, all of the opposing forces had clashed at once, battling for control—or freedom. The forces of good had won out: Farmers were free to work their land. Villagers were free to ply their trades. The hostile mobs that survived had retreated to the Nether and far lands, never really dying out, but relegated to their ugly pursuits under cover of darkness. The fringe types—like Frida and Stormie and Turner—had chosen to live on the edge, doing what it took to stay a step ahead of hostiles. All of the passives and neutrals owed their very lives to one man, the man who had led the victorious charge against evil.

Jools stopped rubbing Beckett's neck abruptly. "There is one fellow. . . ."

A ray of hope glimmered in Rob's eyes. "Who?"

"His name is Colonel M."

CHAPTER 7

"**C**OLONEL M!" FRIDA EXCLAIMED. "THE MAN'S a legend. He's the one who single-handedly fought off the zombie Infinity Brigade!"

"And sent the Ender Dragon to the Void!" Kim added reverently.

"But that was ages ago," Aswan pointed out. "I heard the colonel had retired to the Nether."

"I heard he'd turned explorer and was looking for a way out of the Overworld," said Turner.

"I met him once," Jools said. "But only virtually. I'm not even certain he still has a body."

"It doesn't sound like he needs one," Rob said, admiration in his voice.

"So, how would we find him?" Kim asked.

Only Stormie—Overworld traveler, boundary hopper, and all-around tough girl—had been awed into silence at the mention of the great First War commander. Now she spoke up. "No one locates Colonel M." She paused. "He locates you."

Aswan grinned impishly. "But a . . . *friend* with an extensive social network might be able to uncover his whereabouts."

Rob felt a surge of hope. Could this epic warrior be found to help with their dilemma? Or was he just a myth made of memories and wishful thinking?

"Tell me more about the First War," he said. "It would be better if history didn't repeat itself."

"Amen, brother," Turner said and launched into tales of betrayal, mayhem, and destruction.

Rob put two and two together. "So, there was once a unified people, but then, one day, some splinter groups tried to take over? Like a civil war? Neighbor against neighbor, brother against brother."

"And sister against sister," Frida said. "It started a long history of warrior women in my family. The boys were sent away young, but survival skills were handed down, mother to daughter, for generations."

That explained Frida's loner status, Rob thought. *No wonder she's so defensive. In a good way.*

"If there's a chance of all that coming back around again," Frida said, "I'm all for fighting back."

"Me, too," Stormie and Kim agreed.

Rob eyed the guys.

"Oh, I'm all for that," Jools said, spreading his hands. "As long as I don't have to get killed and respawned over and over. That gets so tedious."

"Hear, hear," Turner chimed in. "It's not the dying I'm so worried about. I just don't want to end up with an empty war chest."

Rob tightened his lips. "In other words, what's in it for you?"

"Hey. A guy's gotta make a living. Especially if he wants to *stay* living. . . ."

Kim stood up. "I think we can all agree on one thing: the only acceptable Overworld is a free Overworld. Right?"

Her remark was met with nods or grunts.

Kim clapped her pink hands. "Then let's get busy defending it!"

*

They set off at dawn the next morning, bidding a woeful Aswan good-bye. "I'll see what I can do about finding your mystery man!" he called to Kim as she teleported off through the burnt crust of the village streets.

Turner stopped by the fletcher's shop on the way out of town to trade for any flints or feathers that had escaped Dr. Dirt's sweep. "We're gonna need 'em," he said, returning with a small stack for everyone's inventory. Jools tried to wave them away, but the others assured him he should be safe rather than sorry.

"I'm not certain that's a possibility," he argued, accepting the crafting ingredients anyway.

Rob could see that he was going to have his work cut out for him to cultivate the mind-set and work ethic needed to get a decent cavalry unit off the ground. At least they'd have a good place to train out on the mesa, with no distractions.

The group rode off toward the other end of the plains, itemizing their supplies and deciding what to conserve and where they might look to find more of what they'd need in the days ahead.

"Jools," Rob said, riding Saber alongside him and Beckett who, in turn, were following Stormie on Armor. "I'm making you quartermaster. You'll be responsible for the supply chain."

Turner heard this and urged Duff to their side, leaving Frida to bring up the rear. "Now wait just a—"

"Give it up, Meat," Frida broke in. "Too many cooks spoil the war." She and Ocelot passed Turner and joined Stormie up front.

Rob grinned. "Key to any army's success: chain of command. We might as well iron it out now, if I'm going to be your captain."

There was silence from the others.

"Doesn't *have* to be me. . . ." Rob added, deflated.

"Yes, it does!" Stormie said, coming to his defense. "Frida's right, Meat. You put one man in charge, and the rest follow him, no questions asked. Otherwise, we're toast." Armor snorted as if in agreement.

"Besides," Kim said, "Rob here knows more about horses—and probably more about cavalry—than any of the rest of us."

"Even you, O bronc whisperer?" Jools teased.

Kim sank in mid-teleport and slid onto Beckett's back behind him. "Even me. I'm self-taught. Rob's a professional."

Rob ducked his chin and studied Saber's withers.

"Yeah, professional moron," Turner said under his breath and trotted on ahead to catch up with the girls.

"Come on, now," Kim said. "All for one, and one for all, and all that jazz."

"I think we need a name!" Stormie said. "Something that will strike fear into the hearts of our enemies."

Jools watched Turner listing in his saddle before him like a dinghy caught in a current. "How about 'Rob's Green Riders'?" he joked.

"Only one of us is green," Turner said, pointing at Frida, clearly missing the slight.

She glared at him, misinterpreting his misinterpretation. "What about 'Big, Fat Jerks'?"

Rob ignored the bickering. "No, it's got to be 'Battalion something'. . . ."

"Yeah, 'Battalion Zero,'" Turner cracked.

"Hey. Actually, I like it!" Rob said.

"It does have the ring of doom," Jools remarked.

"Battalion Zero to the rescue!" cried Stormie, steering Armor behind Rob and Saber.

The others, all except Turner, fell in with the game and guided their horses into file.

"Don't be a party pooper!" Kim called.

"Yeah, come on, Meat!" Stormie goaded him.

He looked over his shoulder at the ragged line of horse soldiers and softened. "That's *Sergeant* Meat to you, Private," he replied as Duff slowed, bringing up the rear without any signal from his rider. Like all smart horses, Duff was well versed in the chain of command.

*

Stormie suggested they cover as much ground that day as possible. "That way, we can deal with the plains boundary tomorrow when it's light out."

So, against everyone's normal instincts, they kept riding as dusk came on.

Kim asked Turner what it was like to work as a paid bodyguard.

"I like the term *bouncer* better. It's kinder." He underscored this by reaching down with his sword and whacking a zombie that had spawned next to the trail. "Bodyguarding is the same as keeping yourself alive, only more lucrative," Turner continued. "Lots of folks don't like to pay for it, though. I've had more than one guy try to stiff me." He took out another zombie. "That's when bodyguarding takes on a whole new meaning. Now, I don't condone killing—" He switched hands and impaled a third zombie on Duff's other side. "—but if it's a choice between you or me, well, you're going down, and that's all there is to it."

He slowed Duff as a baby zombie wobbled toward them. "Hello, little ugly monster," Turner cooed. "Are you . . . *lost?*" He cut the baby zombie's head clean off.

Kim teleported behind them, picking up bits of rotten flesh and the pile of mini potatoes that the baby zombie had dropped.

"What about you, Jools?" Kim asked. "How did you get into the detail business?"

"Observation," he responded. "I'm like you: self-taught. I've just always had an eye for patterns, ever since I was a lad. And the thing about patterns is, deviations can be a matter of life and death. That makes what *I* do lucrative."

"Did you get your start during the First War?" Rob asked.

"That was way before my spawning time," Jools said. "No, as they say, there's always a conflict somewhere in the world at any given moment. Labor strikes, political coups, corporate takeovers—I've just made it my business to find them . . . and to not get involved."

"So, what's different this time?" Turner asked.

Jools thought a moment. "What's different is—I'm not sure there will be a next time after this time—if you get my drift."

Turner nodded solemnly.

The farther they rode from civilization, the fewer hostiles they encountered.

"Zombies may not be bright, but they're predictable," Frida said. "They especially like well-populated areas. They're opportunists, same as the rest of us."

"Hey, speak for yourself," Turner said, offended.

Frida grinned. "You, my friend, are the biggest opportunist of all."

"That's why I'm designating you sergeant at arms," Rob told Turner. "You'll know when to take the offensive—could be against the enemy, could be to maintain order if there's a mutiny in our unit."

"What if he's the one to start the mutiny?" Jools asked.

Turner pulled an innocent face. "I'll have you know, I am as loyal as the day is long."

Stormie waved at the horizon. "Yeah, well, day's about over."

"Good point." Turner pulled Duff up and dismounted. "I say we make camp here."

Rob shook his head. "I didn't release you, Sergeant. Now get back on that horse."

Turner eyed him to see if he meant it. Everyone else waited to see what Turner would do. Slowly, he put a foot back in the stirrup and got back on Duff.

After about a dozen strides, Rob put a hand up. "And, halt!" He gazed around the empty plains. A line of rock outcrops rose in the distance. "Looks like the biome border's not far ahead. We'll make camp here for the night."

"Point taken," Jools murmured, and they all broke formation and set about tending to the horses.

As Rob and Frida crafted some fences together, she touched his arm and said in a low voice, "You don't want to start anything with Turner, you know. He's the deadliest individual I've ever met, at least on the good side of the Overworld."

Rob put down the sticks he was handling. "And we need *deadly* on *our* side. It's time for me to set some rules if I'm going to lead this cavalry." Seeing her grave face, he added, "Don't worry, Frida. He'll come around."

"Yeah, but watch your back. Sometimes he comes around like a boomerang."

Rob felt a pang of worry, but he realized the luxury of showing it was over for him. He'd read that being a commander was a lonely job. Still, that didn't mean he couldn't line up some allies. Frida, he could trust.

"You know this world better than I do," he admitted. "I'll be counting on you to keep your finger on the pulse of . . . everything. You'll be our vanguard. You're the best at scoping out a situation, even before it happens."

"You mean, you want me to be a spy?"

"Call it what you want. It'll be your job to scout things out and draw the battle lines—even if they're inside the battalion."

"I'm not sure I want that job."

He paused. "Somebody's got to do it. It's for the good of the unit."

"And the good of the Overworld." Frida made up her mind. "Count me in."

They finished hooking together fence panels and got the horses settled inside the corral. Saber raised his head, looking meaningfully at Rob from the inside as he shut the gate behind him.

"I know, buddy. It's just for show. Set a good example, will you? I can use all the help I can get."

CHAPTER 8

THE FOLLOWING MORNING, THE MEMBERS OF Battalion Zero mounted up and crossed over from the plains to Bryce Mesa uneventfully. Dr. Dirt's griefers must have been busy elsewhere, sorting through their plunder, while their legions retreated into darkness for the day. Rob couldn't help but breathe a sigh of relief as Saber stepped from turf to clay, putting the boundary behind them. Dead bush and cactus gave way to prairie grass, and the trail began to climb. The small party of riders could have been out for an everyday ride.

The new landscape, though nearly void of trees, offered an endless variety in colors and textures: Flatlands were rimmed by towering stalagmites of clay-covered sandstone, striped by mineral deposits, and interspersed by blue tributaries. Green cacti stood out in relief against the red, orange, and silver rock palette. It was as though the small troop had ridden into an enormous sand painting. And it made Rob more homesick than ever.

His ranch lay in the high desert, in a place not so different from this one, yet a world away . . . somewhere. Although they had gained elevation, Stormie explained that their vantage point couldn't match the altitude of the extreme hills. Still, Rob hoped he might glimpse a landmark that would point the way home.

"Emerald for your thoughts," Kim said to the quiet cowboy as she teleported alongside him.

"Well, I—" He emerged from his reverie and tucked his emotions away. It was up to Rob to rally his soldiers around their shared goal—saving *this* world. His new status as cavalry commander would not allow him to share his longing for home. "I . . . was just thinking how much we have to do to build a base camp," he said.

"What can I do to help?"

"Things are about to heat up for our equine friends, here. I'm naming you master of horses, Kim. We'll need you to keep them fed, healthy, and ready for battle." She nodded. "It's what I do best."

"I'll also want you to act as my ground crew during drills. We'll have to get started training these recruits as horse soldiers, as well as training the horses to work together." He knew that Kim's keen eye could come in handy.

"While I'm at it, I might as well divvy up the rest of the duties." He called to the others, "Gather around, players!"

Rob explained that they would be fortifying a safe camp and preparing a defensive strategy as soon as they found a suitable location. "Frida will ride ahead with Stormie to scout one out and update our map. Once we get where we're going, everyone will have to take the initiative to fulfill their tasks. Turner, you'll do as you see fit to keep swords, bows, arrows, and axes available to the rest of us. Jools will watch our food and health levels and make sure we have enough vittles, milk, fuel, and other supplies. He'll also assist me in drawing up our battle plans."

Turner hit his palm with his fist and Jools nodded.

"I've put Kim in charge of the horses, and she'll help Frida get grass and sugar for them."

"What'll I do?" Stormie asked.

"I've been thinking about the day we first met. When you blew Lady Craven out of the water. Do you still have that TNT cannon?"

"Sure do."

"Then you'll be our artillery commander."

"Anything that can be made with gunpowder will be made with gunpowder, *sir!*" she said, snapping off a salute.

"We'll all have to chip in as additional duties arise," Rob told the group. "We might have to set a night guard. . . . We'll see."

"Wish I had some brushes and dyes," Stormie mused. "This scenery is awesome."

"You paint?" Kim asked.

"In my nonexistent spare time."

Turner sidled up to her on Duff. "Hey, if we do get some time off, maybe you could do a likeness of me." He showed her his profile. "I promised Sundra something to remember me by."

"You mean, other than a lingering odor?" Jools remarked.

"All right, all right," Rob scolded. "We're supposed to be forming a unit, not starting a civil war."

"Ain't nothing civil about him," Turner grumbled.

"Sergeant! Let it go," Rob rebuked him. "The world is depending on us. We're a cavalry now. Let's act like one."

*

At Frida's suggestion, the budding battalion made camp on the lee side of a rugged, red cliff studded with rock spires that seemed to shoot up toward the moon.

"Looka them hoodoos," Turner said, admiring their tall, striped beauty.

"They're almost like sentries," Kim remarked.

"They are, in a way," Rob said. "We'll use them as a natural fence."

Frida studied the rock towers. "I can plant cacti in between them to seal marauders out."

"Or keep us in," Jools noted. "I died once from touching a cactus. But then, I rarely wear armor, so it was my own fault."

"Well, that's going to change," Rob said. "Desert or no desert, I want everyone in body armor during drill." He eyed Jools. "And we'll all participate."

Jools was taken aback. "But—"

Rob broke in. "I'm not asking you to fight, Quartermaster. I am asking you to be ready to fight if push comes to shove."

Jools absorbed this idea, but at least he didn't argue.

"Besides, you're a fit rider. I think you'll enjoy the mounted drills. And working with the group might motivate Beckett to get the lead out."

Jools cracked a smile. "Nothing like a good gallop, I always say."

They staked out their camp next to a stream, with a clump of dead bushes for shade. Jools set up his crafting table and supply chest. Turner inventoried their weaponry and ammunition. Then they all took a break, enjoying a lunch of pork chop jerky, which did a great deal to ease the earlier group tension. As their food bars filled, they chatted busily about their duty rosters. The horses found a sandpit to roll in before stretching out to bask in the sun.

When the hoodoo rimrocks began to cast afternoon shadows, the time came for their first drill. The cavalry donned their armor and outfitted the horses. Rob asked Kim to mine some hardened clay and place the blocks end to end to make an oblong arena. A few of the others busted up some sand blocks and lined the inside of the area with sand. Kim, looking businesslike in her pink iron helmet, called for them all to wrangle their horses and file in. They then spent more time than it should have taken to form a line facing Rob and Saber. Their leader intended to give them a short demonstration of some of the more advanced moves they could look forward to.

"Kim! Can I borrow your earring?"

Rob hung the gold hoop from a long, twiggy stick he'd pulled from his inventory and stuck into the ground at one end of the arena. Next, he rode Saber to the opposite end and drew his new sword. "Somebody say *charge*," he instructed.

Kim put up a hand. "Charge!"

Saber took off at a mad gallop, heading straight for the target.

As they neared, Rob made ready to stab with his sword and capture the earring. Perhaps he should have talked this over with Saber first. At the last second, the horse swerved directly at the stick and—thinking it was an obstacle—gave a mighty leap to clear it. He did . . . leaving his surprised rider behind.

In an all too familiar way, Rob found himself tumbling through space and landing abruptly on a pile of sand. *At least there aren't any zombies waiting for me this time,* he thought wryly, feeling more like a rickety skeleton than he ever had before.

"And that move would serve what purpose in battle?" Jools asked with mock sincerity.

"I think Rob's showing us how *not* to do it, y'all," Stormie said in his defense. "Right?"

"Uh, yeah." He smiled sheepishly and got up from the hard ground. "Let that be a lesson. Even the most experienced rider can fall. And look where you want to go. Don't expect your horse to know what you're thinking! "

"At least Duff won't have to worry about that," Jools needled Turner. "'Nature abhors a vacuum.'"

"People! Another lesson." Rob put his foot in the saddle stirrup and remounted Saber. "If you fall, you have to get right back on." He wheeled Saber around and performed the earring maneuver again, this time legging the horse firmly to the left and keeping his head down until *after* his sword had successfully grabbed the golden earring.

This prompted a smattering of applause from the onlookers, and even Turner conceded that the exercise was a good form of target practice.

"When you can send an arrow through that earring, you'll really have something going," Rob said. "Now. Enough of the preview. We're going to get you all cantering and the horses comfortable in close formation."

Carnival music would have been a good accompaniment for the chaos that followed, which lasted until Rob and Kim worked out the proper lineup for the horses. Beckett was too slow to be in front. Armor was too antsy to be in the rear. Ocelot didn't yet understand the need to travel in a straight line, and until she did, Frida fell off again and again when gravity overcame the horse's sinuous movements. To everyone's surprise, Turner and Duff were the stars of the show wherever they were placed in the order.

When Rob mentioned this to Kim, she replied, "That's why I chose Duff for him. That horse is a born babysitter."

Turner was outraged, of course, but Rob knew what Kim meant. Some horses just naturally take care of their riders. In this case, it made Turner appear to have far more skill than he really did. Rob used the illusion in his favor. "Babysitter . . . What she means is, Turner will obviously pass on excellent horseback riding genes."

"No doubt, Sundra will be pleased," Jools commented.

At last the entire group was able to ride at a canter, and Rob and Kim had figured out the order that kept the horses happiest: Armor in the lead, followed by Ocelot, then Duff, then Beckett, and last, Saber. This would allow Rob to keep an eye on everyone and ride the boss horse in to help if anyone got into trouble.

Next, Captain Rob, as Stormie was calling him, fell out of line and split the others into pairs. He had Armor and Duff canter in a circle in one direction and Ocelot and Beckett in the other, passing each other at their right shoulders. Of course, Ocelot veered out, and Turner forgot which side was his right side, and they enjoyed several near misses that left Frida and Stormie on the ground.

Rob insisted that they keep repeating the drill until they got it right. But after half a dozen go-arounds, the women were getting frustrated and the men were getting bored. Rob responded to their whining by tightening the proverbial reins. "Again!" he commanded. "With feeling this time."

Another three tries and three more commands brought the troopers to the edge of their patience—which Rob ignored.

He might have had a goal in mind, but Kim could see that an early grave was more likely. As Rob balled

his fists and made to berate the group again, she teleported over to him and settled on Saber's rump.

"Begging your pardon, sir," she whispered in Rob's
ear. "They may be soldiers, but they are players first.
Think back. What was it that you wanted when that
creeper blew up your sand pillar? Or when those zombies caught fire in the sunlight?"

She jarred him back to that first day in this new
world. "I wanted to know what the heck was going
on," he answered, tight-lipped.

She clapped him on the shoulder with a pink
palm. "You wanted to know *why*." She waved at the
riders, who were clearly not pleased with the situation. "Orders are orders, but if you want your commands to be followed, you'd best explain why. They're
like smart horses. Nobody wants to follow a blind
lead."

Rob took a deep breath. She was right. The group
had no idea why he wanted them to go through these
exercises.

"Thanks, Kim. Sometimes I need a second set of
eyes to see what's really going on."

"Just doing my ground crew duty, sir," she replied
graciously and teleported back toward Frida to help
her up from the dirt.

"Okay, players," Rob called. "Come over here
and line up in front of me." He waited, letting them

straighten out their ranks on their own instead of at his instruction. Then he gave them the rationale for circling toward each other at a canter—it got the horses used to an enemy charging at them. Passing on the right prepared the riders for sword combat with oncoming hostiles.

"But I'm left-handed," Turner said.

"Doesn't matter; your enemy might not be. Get used to it."

"Now, let's try the same pattern at a trot," Rob said. "That'll make it easier to nail. We want to end this drill on a good note. That's how horses learn they did the right thing."

And men, Rob thought, meaning himself. If his very first mounted drill went south, he could kiss his leadership good-bye.

*

Rob's strategy worked, and the riders succeeded in performing several head-on loops at a trot. "We'll get it at a canter next time," he assured them, surprising himself with another familiar sentiment. *Of course! That's how I bring the young horses along back on the ranch—a step at a time.* There were a lot of similarities between horses and humans—things that he had never seen before, because he hadn't needed to. He reminded himself that less could be more, at least in the early stages of training.

So he let Frida hold off on a full survey of the area until the next day. That night, when Jools suggested running a trip wire around their camp instead of rotating a night watch, Rob agreed. They were all exhausted.

By the time everyone had rubbed down and fed their horses and secured the perimeter, about all they could manage to do was light a campfire and chew on some dry chicken jerky. Even Turner sat idle after supper, not sharpening his weapon blades or counting his stash of emeralds. Tired as he was, Rob couldn't help but enjoy this lull before the coming storm.

It would have to be a solitary pleasure.

He wanted to sit next to Stormie by the stream and hear more about her career choice or join Kim in cooing baby talk to the horses. He wouldn't even mind trading insults with Jools and Turner or asking Frida for advice about . . . everything. But fraternizing with the other players might lessen their perception of him as a leader. While Rob understood that it was important to maintain their respect, he was unsure how he'd fare in the thick of a real battle. He had weapons, he had soldiers, but he wasn't sure he had their trust. Maybe he could cultivate it with an awesome plan . . . which he also didn't have.

Something Kim had said earlier, though, made him realize he couldn't just wait for something to happen. He'd have to jump in feetfirst. Like that first night, after the creeper had exploded his sand pillar, Rob had rebuilt the tower first and asked questions later. It had kept him alive. Yep, a guy could read about leading a cavalry all he wanted, but the only way to learn what worked was to do it.

"Jools, Stormie," Rob called to his quartermaster and artillery commander. "We need to put our heads together first thing tomorrow. Come up with an initial target and strategy. Bring your map, Stormie," he added as an afterthought.

"Kim, can you hook up with Aswan on chat and see if he scored any intel on that Colonel M?" If anyone could help them with strategy, Rob was sure it was the war veteran. "Frida, in the meantime, I'll need you to scout out the immediate area for resources."

Everyone agreed. It felt good to have friends Rob could count on.

"And Turner . . ." Rob said. "Turner?" he repeated when he got no reply.

He looked over both shoulders. "Has anyone seen Turner?"

No one had.

The horses were quiet. The mercenary wasn't among them.

There were no moans of zombies, rattles of skeletons, or bellicose proclamations by griefer dictators to suggest that their sergeant at arms had been killed or captured.

They all got up and searched as far as the illumination from the campfire would allow them. Turner was nowhere to be found. And, upon inspection, it became clear . . . the trip wire hadn't been tripped.

CHAPTER 9

FATIGUE WAS FORGOTTEN IN THE WAKE OF Turner's disappearing act. Rob ordered Jools to dispense torches so they could form a search party. But Jools returned from the supply chest with troubling news.

"My potions have been messed with. And some of my night vision elixir is missing!" He quickly handed out torches. Everyone suited up with armor from their inventories.

"Let's stick together!" Rob ordered. "Frida. Is there anywhere inside the trip wire that you haven't scouted yet?"

She waved toward the eastern quadrant, at some squat outcrops.

Rob mentally kicked himself, filing away the knowledge that exhaustion was no excuse to delay a thorough examination of the terrain. "This way!" He led the group, torches bobbing in the darkness. "Turner!" he called, and the rest echoed him. If there were hostiles out there, silence would be no protection.

They came across a sandy spot and, suddenly, Frida's keen eyes spied a clue. "Footprints!" she said. "And here's an entrance in the rock!"

She and Stormie went in first and then beckoned the rest of the group. They entered a windowless room with a dirt floor. Three arched doorways led deeper into the cliffside.

Frida knelt to examine the ground more closely. "More footprints here. He—or someone—went this-a-way!"

Rob gulped as they entered a dark corridor. Sure, he had done some spelunking in the caves on the outskirts of his ranch. But that had been in his known world . . . not one where explanations seemed to follow trouble—sometimes too late.

He tiptoed after Frida and Stormie. Jools and Kim crept behind him, their torches revealing curtains of cobwebs hanging from the ceiling and chunks of old railway track at their feet. "A mine shaft," Rob stated.

"Watch out for cave spiders," Frida called. "They're poisonous!"

Rob's scalp tingled beneath his helmet, and he lashed out instinctively with his sword.

"Hey, watch it!" Jools said, jumping sideways.

"Sorry."

They descended a staircase that ran along the patchy rail system, stepping over old mine carts and collapsed pillars. This would be no place to get trapped if the roof caved in, Rob thought, now worried for his cranky friend. "Turner!" he called out, his voice reverberating off the walls.

The passageway angled ninety degrees to the right. After Rob had made the turn, he heard a shout from Kim behind him.

"Our torches went out!"

He wheeled around and rushed back, just as Jools cried, *"Aaugh!"*

The blaze from Rob's torch revealed that a cave spider had landed squarely on the quartermaster's head.

"He's got me!"

Before anyone else could react, Kim had drawn her pink sword. "Die! Die! Die!" she screamed and whacked the creature a deathblow. It thumped to the ground next to Jools, who lay motionless.

Rob stood helplessly as the small girl replaced the sword in her inventory and dusted off her hands. Frida and Stormie retraced their steps and appeared at the corner, supplying two extra torches from their stash. But there was nothing they could do to help Jools. No one had any milk.

"He'll come out of it pretty soon," Kim said nonchalantly, stooping to pick up the string the cave spider had dropped. "Hey! Dead spider eye!" she said. "Five points!"

A hand reached over her shoulder and snatched the eye. "I'll take that," Jools said, already back to normal. "Just what I need for my brewing inventory."

Rob shuddered, suppressing the urge to run screaming back up the stairs and out into the night. He had never been afraid of spiders or the dark before . . . but that had been when he could predict what was around the next corner. He steeled himself and rounded the bend again with the others, calling out to Turner.

*

The staircase seemed to descend forever, and then, abruptly, it bottomed out. The downward dead end offered two routes: one to the left and one to the right. This caused as much of a stir among the players as the mine shaft's discovery had.

"*Shhh!*" Stormie urged from her place in the lead. "There's something going on up here." From Rob's place behind Frida, he could hear shuffling and snuffling. It sounded like a bear. But even cave bears— which he reminded himself were extinct—wouldn't venture this far below the earth's surface in any world.

The foot soldiers pressed behind Stormie to look as she swept her torch around the corner.

"Who's there!" she challenged.

To their surprise, the creature that swiveled to face them was built like a man—but turned huge, protruding eyes their way.

Rob recognized what he was seeing and pushed past Stormie, ripping at Turner's face. "Safety goggles!" He held them up, feeling weak in the knees. "What do you think you're doing down here?"

Turner reached back with a pickaxe and brandished it, stopping short of using it on his commander. At that moment, Jools pressed through and tossed a splash potion at him.

As though anesthetized with elephant tranquilizer, Turner's eyes rolled back in his head. He swayed, dropped the pickaxe, and crumpled, lurching forward with outstretched hands, preparing to strangle whoever had surprised him.

"Na na, can't catch me," teased Jools, dancing just out of his reach.

Now by the light of several torches, Turner's eyes reflected disbelief, then understanding, then rage.

"Custom blend," Jools explained. "Slowness plus weakness plus annoyance. That last one is an exclusive."

While Turner reeled about, Frida assessed the scene. "He's been mining! Look—ore strikes galore, and a mine cart with a chest half-full. Diamonds, lapis, emeralds, and more. . . . Someone abandoned this mine way too soon."

Rob leaned over with his torch. "But how could he see what he was doing?"

Jools rubbed his chin. "My night vision potion, remember? Those goggles were for protection, not for seeing in the dark."

Rob nodded grimly. "That means he planned this."

Kim glared at Turner. "You should be ashamed of yourself!"

Frida shook her head at the renegade. "I am super, super disappointed in you, Meat."

Turner's voice returned, still affected by the slow-ness spell. "Dis-ap-pointed . . . ? You should—thank me!"

"You want us to believe you were going to share this loot?" Rob said, angry beyond belief.

"Would-n't go . . . that . . . far," Turner replied honestly. "But you're . . . wel-come to mine the . . . other . . . shaft."

"I ought to take a pickaxe to you!" Rob shouted, then forced himself to calm down. "Now. Here's what we're going to do. Frida, Stormie: You see Turner safely back to camp. Keep a blade on him. Kim, Jools: You help me piston this cart up to the surface."

The additional work was not welcome, but the angry adrenaline rush enabled the group to complete the tasks. By and by, they regrouped around the campfire, Turner guarded by the two women.

Rob stood over the dishonored sergeant at arms. "What have you got to say for yourself?"

Turner cleared his throat. "It occurred to me that there might be some dead mines around these parts. There's always a nugget or two left over once the miners have gone home."

"So you just thought you'd go excavating by yourself? In the dark?"

Turner averted his gaze. "Early bird gets the worm," he mumbled.

Kim and Jools pushed the half-loaded mine cart forward. "That's great, guys," Rob said. "Jools, why don't you craft an extra supply chest. We'll store it all in there. And, as of now, everyone shifts their inventory to the quartermaster, outside of what you'd need to get yourself to the village and back."

Turner squealed like a stuck pig. "That loot's mine! Finders keepers." He struggled to rise, but Frida and Stormie held him back.

"All goods are communal until this war is over," Rob declared. "We might need bribe money, and these gemstones will come in handy." Still, he didn't like seeing Turner restrained. "Listen, Sergeant. This will actually put you ahead. By giving up some of your stuff, you lay claim to all of the group's stuff."

That sentiment seemed to cheer Turner up. "I never thought of it like that," he said.

"And if everything goes our way," Stormie put in, "we'll each head home with lots more than we started out with."

Turner thought it over.

"Can we trust you?" Rob asked.

He frowned. "Awright . . . seeing as I have no choice."

"Oh, you have a choice, Turner. It's my way or the highway," Rob said. "And I doubt Dr. Dirt will make you as fair an offer."

Turner knew he was right. "Copy that," he said, and the girls released him.

*

Reality set in the next day like cold rain as the members of Battalion Zero began to fully grasp the magnitude of the burden that they had taken upon themselves. Reconnaissance, strategy, defense—the many aspects of battle preparation kept them busy all morning.

"I'm astonished at how much work it is to start a war," Jools said as he concentrated on setting up a database on his computer. The supply chests were full of so many things that he couldn't keep track of them all. And he didn't want anything else to go missing.

"I reckon that's why armies are always . . . big," Rob mused as he studied Stormie's map, which he'd opened up on top of one of the chests.

He had sent Frida and Turner to scout out supply routes. He wanted someone reliable keeping an eye on Turner. Kim was off spreading hay bales for the horses and checking their feet. If they were going to be galloping over this mesa hardpan their hooves would need lots of attention.

"Stormie, can you start marking the biomes on the map that we know are under Dr. Dirt's control?"

She left the stack of torches she was crafting and joined him. "Well, I know for sure he had a presence at the swampland, roofed forest, and stone beach—and the jungle boundary where we met. Plus, Aswan's intel put his army at the forest, taiga, mountain, and ocean borders. I'm not sure which ocean."

"Turner and Frida said they'd met trouble at the cold taiga, plains, and mesa."

"Which mesa?" Stormie asked, worried.

"Not sure." Rob shrugged. "Guess it wasn't this one."

"So, in other words, it's take your pick," Jools said as he stepped over the pile of torches and came closer. "Eenie meenie miney, biome!" He closed his eyes and stabbed a finger at the map.

"Without knowing how many troops are in any given zone, I guess your guess is as good as mine,"

Rob told him. "Do we want to start with the boundary that offers the best defense, or the one that will do the most good?"

"You mean the most good for other people?" Stormie clarified. "We'll get around to that. We need to knock off the areas that are the most likely to leave us alive and all together."

"Thank you so much for that insight," Jools murmured.

"So . . ." Rob scratched his head. "Ambush with great cover, or advance where our ranks will be able to overwhelm skeleton mobs easily?"

Jools considered the pros and cons. "We could ambush them just after dusk if we find a place where they have to travel single file. Or we could ride at them in a larger, but confined space, allowing them no choice but to retreat." He paused. "Or . . . we could wait until near sunrise and lure them out into the desert far enough that they wouldn't be able to escape before burning to a crisp."

Rob and Stormie eyed him with admiration.

"Let's mull it over awhile," Rob said. "At least those are three options." *And I have no idea which one might succeed,* he said to himself. "Meanwhile, Stormie, keep track of the battle lines that we know about and help Frida scope them out over the next few days."

As he spoke the vanguard's name, she approached from the north with Turner beside her. He held something large and flat over his head. "Leather!" he called happily.

"They must have found some cows," Jools said.

Stormie marveled, "How that man enjoys getting something for free . . ."

But Rob was pleased, too. He had been dreaming of a good, rare steak.

*

Instead, stew headlined the dinner menu. Kim cooked the beef from the cow Turner had killed along with some carrots and potatoes she'd added to the group's inventory.

"This is so good, Kim," Rob said, attacking his plate.

Stormie sighed after swallowing a mouthful. "Just like Mama used to make."

"Thanks, guys. What all did you find, Frida?" Kim asked.

Frida ticked off the potential resources they had spotted in the vicinity of the northern savanna and the adjoining sand desert. There was sugarcane to plant near camp and plenty of acacia trees to bust up for sticks and planks. Frida grinned. "I brought back a mess of wool. Didn't have my shears, so I had to off the sheep to get it. But I know it'll be useful defensively."

Turner nodded. "I see where you're coming from, sister. Stuff burns like lightning."

"Speaking of which," Rob broke in. "Sergeant at Arms, give us a weapons report."

"Well, we can sure use that wool to build a fire line if we need to. We've got a few dozen swords—wood, stone, and iron. Might craft a diamond one with some of what I mined last . . ." he trailed off, not wishing to revisit the painful subject. "Then there's three or four bows apiece and Stormie's TNT cannon. And our axes and pickaxes will do double duty as weapons, once the good stuff wears out."

They all listened solemnly.

"Then there's the fun stuff," Turner said, rubbing his hands together. "Sand. We'll need more—lots of it. We'll stack some up for suffocation traps—always entertaining when zombies are in the mix. And then we'll build some super-nasty pit traps. These'll have a trip wire around the outside, and we'll fill 'em up with cactuses."

Jools grimaced. Rob was glad to have Turner on their side . . . for the time being, anyway.

"Besides the traps, we might tame us up a couple of wolves. They can eat the heck out of a mob of skeletons. And then there's the potions. . . ." He nodded at Jools.

"I've been steadily accumulating brewing ingredients," the quartermaster reported. "So far, right now we've got a couple dozen doses for whatever ails us in battle." He cast a sidelong glance at Turner. "Or in camp, as the case may be."

Turner ignored him. "As far as ammunition goes," he picked up where he'd left off, "we've got a long way to go. We could stand to fill our TNT inventories. I'ma work on as many arrows as I can between now and . . . doomsday."

Rob flinched. "I'll pitch in and help," he offered, nodding at the stack in progress.

The weapons expert gave him a disparaging glance. "Thanks, but no thanks, Newbie—I mean, Cap'n. Well, you can set to crafting bows, if you like, but leave the other to me." He picked up a stick from a stack next to him and flexed it. "A bow is basically a bent stick, but an arrow, well. . . ." He retrieved an arrow from those he had been working on and eyed it admiringly. "An arrow is a work of art."

Again, relief and confidence flooded Rob. Turner would be working for their side. Still, the day's chores had ratcheted the stress level in camp up a notch. Although nobody mentioned it, everyone was silently thinking about their next move. When would they make it? How tough would it be? And would it be successful?

No one really wanted to know the answers.

As they sat around the campfire working on their pet projects, Kim suddenly chirped, "Great news, Battalion Zero!" She checked the screen on her laptop and smiled. "Aswan came through. One of his traders has the coordinates to a Nether fortress where we can find Colonel M."

"Wow!" Frida said. "How does he survive in the Nether?"

Jools knew the answer. "He—or whatever he uses as a skin if he no longer has a body—rides the most awesome steed in all the Overworld. Or the under-world, for that matter." He gave Rob a meaningful stare. "It's said that Nightwind can outrun even the devil himself."

CHAPTER 10

ROB WAS IMPRESSED. THIS COLONEL M WAS A legendary cavalryman—just what they needed to help them devise a rock-solid battle plan.

"There's just one problem," Kim said, tapping her computer. "The trader said the colonel isn't . . . receiving visitors right now."

Turner blew out a breath. "So? We'll go down there and knock on his virtual door. Can't nobody get thrown out of the Nether."

"Perhaps because only an imbecile would willingly spend any time there—other than the colonel, of course," Jools said.

"True," Stormie put in. "But it rocks as a transportation portal. Before I met y'all, I was considering using it myself to avoid Overworld boundary skirmishes."

"It's not exactly a place where you can put your feet up and relax, though," Frida explained to Rob.

"How come?" he asked uneasily.

"Raging lava falls," Turner pointed out.

"And where there's lava, there's blaze mobs," Jools said.

"Ghasts," Stormie spat out. "They'll blow you to kingdom come."

"And don't forget the zombie pigmen!" Kim added.

Rob's eyes widened. "Z-zombie pig—what?"

"You heard right." Kim nodded. "And zombie pigmen could care less about lava."

Rob's head was spinning. Those all sounded like formidable opponents. He tried to put on a brave face. "Well, at least there aren't skeletons! That's a relief." He chuckled weakly.

"Oh, there are," Kim said. "Wither skeletons. Tons of 'em."

Frida noticed Rob's baffled expression. "Captain. Sounds like you need an overview. Okay. Nether 101."

She launched into a description of Colonel M's adopted home. In the underworld, time stood still and maps were of little use. The netherrack terrain was sharp, uneven, and full of holes and trenches. Although traversing it would get you farther along than you could go up on the world surface, netherrack was extremely difficult to navigate. Certain horses and mules might handle it better than human players, though.

"Beckett, for instance, can hold his own," Jools said of his sure-footed horse.

"With a potion of swiftness," Stormie put in, "because you'll probably have to flee from super-fast moving mobs and lava flows."

Turner laced his fingers together and stretched his hands over his head. "And I hope you like fire," he said.

"Who doesn't?" Rob replied faintly.

"Fires generate spontaneously," Turner went on. "*Pow!* Then there's things that set you on fire: lava lakes, blazes, magma cubes. . . ."

"Ugh." Jools shivered. "*Those* fire slimes."

"Doesn't sound too hospitable," Rob concluded. "So, why would anyone move to the Nether?"

Turner's eyes lit up. "Loot! Big time."

Frida scowled at this evidence of her mercenary friend's one-track mind. "Or, in Colonel M's case, no pesky neighbors. The man probably got fed up with the state of the Overworld after all his hard work in the First War."

Rob took this in soberly. If Colonel M had given up on the Overworld, what chance did they have of regaining the peace? Then again, the Nether didn't sound all that hot, either. Or maybe too hot. "Are you sure this Nether isn't home to fire-breathing dragons?" he asked.

Jools stared at him like he was crazy. "You're thinking of the End. That's where the Ender Dragon lives."

Stormie put a hand on Rob's elbow. "But don't worry. They don't breathe fire."

"Yeah, just acid," Turner put in. "But that don't concern you. I'd say your biggest worry in the Nether ain't *whether* you're gonna burn up, but *how*."

This seeped into Rob's consciousness like cement into foam rubber. Forget spiders and the pitch-dark; a flaming underworld was definitely something he *was* afraid of.

And in no way could he admit that to this group.

*

The captain of Battalion Zero sidestepped his fears by focusing on practical matters instead. "We can't afford the time and resources it would take to visit the Nether," he informed the players. "Besides getting there and risking manpower and horses, we'd still have to persuade Colonel M that our cause is worthy. And that's a long shot."

Kim's face fell. Frida, Stormie, and Turner seemed just as disheartened. Only Jools looked pleased.

"That's not to say we won't consult him in the future," Rob assured them, crossing his fingers behind his back.

This appeared to restore Stormie's faith in him. "I get it. Keep him in your hip pocket," she said. "Like an old boyfriend. Or a secret weapon."

"Yeah. A secret weapon," Rob echoed, thinking how badly they needed one—but one that might not cost them so much to acquire.

In the next few days, the troopers worked on their training and filling their supply slots. At the next drill Rob showed them how to bombproof their horses.

"Ya mean, so creepers can't damage 'em?" Turner asked.

Rob regarded him with amusement. "It's an expression. Means that nothing can scare them." He walked down the line of horses and soldiers. "I've noticed that these animals are used to seeing zombies and other nonanimal and nonhuman mobs. But what happens if they have to brush up against them? Or charge them?"

Stormie understood. "Armor's brave, but he's not that brave," she said.

So they spent some time desensitizing the horses to uncommon things that they might experience. Rob put skeleton bones in a sack and shook them to make noise as he made his way around the arena. Stormie set off small charges from her TNT cannon as the horses trotted past. Frida got down off of Ocelot and put some meat that had been out in the sun too long in her pockets, then impersonated a zombie's staggering walk and guttural wail.

"We know horses can see green," Rob informed the group, motioning at Frida and the skin color she shared with zombies. "That's how they can spot grass when they're too far away to smell it."

Frida's impersonation was so accurate that Ocelot whirled around, resisting, when she tried to remount.

"It's working!" Rob shouted. He knew that they wanted to initiate the behavior they were trying to eliminate in horses, or the de-spooking would never take. So he had her attempt to mount all the other horses, Saber included.

In the drills that followed, they practiced skirmishing from horseback as well as dismounting and fighting on foot. Turner and the others found the full-length bows too clumsy to handle from the saddle.

"I can modify these," the weapons expert said. Sure enough, the next day, he provided shorter bows that he'd reinforced with cave spider webbing. They were both strong and easy to maneuver over their horses' withers, allowing the soldiers to shoot from either side.

"I reckon we've learned everything we need to know to take Dr. Dirt's army," Turner said after they'd become adept at hitting targets from horseback.

"It's a start," Rob told him. "Now we've got to practice working as a team."

This would be difficult for everybody. If there was one thing each battalion member shared, it was a self-sufficient streak. It was what allowed them to survive: Kim, alone on the plains at her ranch; Jools, a mastermind among warmongers; Frida, Stormie, and Turner, each bent on a solitary quest for personal gain. Their independence was their greatest strength . . . and their greatest weakness. "In battle," Rob explained, "acting together makes the unit stronger than any one player. That's why you see a line of cavalry soldiers charging abreast, not in single file."

"Lots more effective," Jools agreed.

"Considering we'd have a girl in front," Turner commented.

"Can it, Meat," Stormie warned him.

He looked her over. "Wish I could," he quipped.

Frida hauled off and hit him in the jaw.

"I'm glad you demonstrated that, Vanguard," Rob said, holding back a laugh as Turner rubbed his face. "It's time for hand-to-hand practice. And all we've got to practice on is each other."

The suggestion was not completely out of line. Frida and Turner had long been sparring partners, and the rest had experienced plenty of melee attacks. In a short time, they were paired off and throwing each other around the arena, pulling no punches. Jools had set up a healing station with various helpful potions and some snacks, which would help strengthen their health bars.

At last Rob stood back and watched his troops display real skill, on and off their horses. On the ground, they could thrust and parry, feint and lunge, and just plain fight dirty with their teeth if they had to. Mounted, the group could now ride at the same speed in the same direction. They rode boot to boot, without leaving enough space between each other for enemy combatants to attack. They could move their line forward, turn as one, and stop on command— this last one, an important detail. Although he wished he could draw this training out forever, Rob couldn't deny that Battalion Zero was about as ready as it would ever be to hit the front lines.

Kim teleported over and nudged him. "Looks good, huh, Captain?"

He nodded.

But would *good* be good enough?

*

Rob and his advisers, Jools and Stormie, agreed that their first advance on Dr. Dirt and company would be close to camp, allowing for a quick retreat. "Or a quick victory party," Stormie remarked.

Their vanguard had identified a mountainous roofed forest to the northeast where the mesa and savanna intersected. "The cliffs on one side will be too tall for skeletons to scale, but our sure-footed horses can use them as a last-resort getaway," Frida had said.

Jools liked that the light level beneath the dense canopy would be low enough for them to strike during the day, when they could fight fresh. "Dirt's mobs will have the advantage at night," he mentioned. "And we'll have the option to retreat to the desert due south of there, bringing them out into sunlight." He eyed Stormie and Rob. "I've run it through my probability calculator. It gives us an 85 percent chance of winning."

Rob sucked in a breath. "Or a 15 percent chance of losing."

"What about a tie?" Stormie joked, trying to keep things light.

As they worked up a strategy, Turner, Frida, and Kim undertook the dangerous side trip of capturing and taming some wolves. They faded into the flatland forest just east of their mesa camp, planning to either go undetected by mobs or to subdue them if their numbers were small. The wolves would help them attack Dirt's skelemobs and hunt down witches, which dropped valuable gunpowder. Their TNT stores were extremely low, and it would take as much gunpowder as they could secure to make more TNT to charge their cannon.

These tasks were accomplished in a few days. Kim's deftness at charming animals, plus a few skeleton bones they'd picked up, netted them two loyal wolves, which they named Thing 1 and Thing 2. The group located three witch huts in the swampland at the other edge of the forest, and Frida's and Turner's exceptional aim with bow and arrow allowed them to kill two dozen witches without getting close enough to be popped by their splash potions.

When the three troopers returned to camp, their spirits were high.

"We are unstoppable!" Turner declared.

"Then *you* go fight Dirt's army," Jools suggested. "I'll stay here and play games on my computer."

Rob did not take this jest well. "You'll pack our supply chests to the battlefront as planned, Quartermaster." He threw Jools a bone. "You can keep a wolf with you on guard until we need it, though."

Jools approved of this idea and so did Thing 1. He'd bounded up to beg for the skeleton rib. "Nice doggie," Jools said, patting the silver-brown wolf's head.

Stormie spent the rest of the day crafting TNT, while the others polished armor and horse tack and washed up in the stream. "I run a clean unit," Rob proclaimed, believing the account he had read in an old war manual that a well-turned-out battalion was more fearsome in the enemies' eyes.

At last there was nothing more to be done than get a good night's sleep before mounting their attack the next day. Rob wasn't one for prayer, but he did believe in the support of a good friend. He went to visit Saber in the horse enclosure before climbing into his bedroll.

Saber stood with his head drooping, somewhere between dozing and waking.

"Well, buddy. Tomorrow's the big day," Rob said.

Saber swished his tail.

"All I ask is that you watch where you put your feet and follow your heart over every jump."

The horse shivered to shake off a modified fly. Then Saber nuzzled Rob's shoulder.

"I will, too, Saber. I will, too."

With that, the castaway cowboy-turned-cavalry commander headed for bed . . . but not for sleep.

*

No one said more than absolutely necessary the next morning as they made ready to leave camp. Armored, loaded, and mounted, Battalion Zero moved out, with Kim riding behind Rob on Saber to ensure she wouldn't be left behind.

Their plan was to cross the mountainous border, which would likely be undefended, and then overtake the enemy inside the roofed forest near its eastern flank. The horses obliged, taking them over the mesa's high points between hoodoos and dropping into the mountain steps, with the two wolves trotting alongside.

"I feel like a sitting duck," Turner mumbled as they descended the rock terrace, easily visible from the forest cover below.

"And so you are," Jools said. "This is where Kim and I get off." They would fall back with the extra supplies and horse equipment, and this would be the rendezvous point after . . . whatever happened.

Thing 1 sat down next to Jools and Beckett, his tongue hanging out and tail wagging.

Kim slid off Saber and raised a fist. "Go get 'em, Bat Zero!"

"Tally ho!" Stormie called, and she led the rest of the riders and the second wolf into the unknown.

At first they heard and saw nothing down in the dark confines of the forest, which offered glimpses only through rare pockets of sparse foliage. As they approached, however, they heard the low moans of zombies and, later, the distinctive jangle of bones.

"Dirt won't risk a fire in that closed-in forest," Frida whispered. "So no creepers. We've got that going for us."

Rob knew they were as prepared as they could be to ward off zombie and skeleton attacks. He itched under his iron chest plate, and then was glad for the distraction. This caused him to be a hair late in drawing his bow.

Ka-chang! An arrow glanced off his armor just as the riders hit the forest floor.

"Ready, battalion!" he cried, wildly searching for the attacker. His eyes had not yet adjusted to the gloom. *Thang! Prang! Th-oop!* Arrows sailed all around him, and the sound of jittering bones grew louder.

"Forward, march . . . charge!"

Turner and Stormie fitted arrows to bows. Frida set Thing 2 loose. Together they rode forward, but immediately the trees in their path broke up their ranks. Rob urged Saber around one oak and then forward, and they leapt a giant mushroom, straight at a pair of armored skeletons.

Rob could barely swallow. His shot at a skull missed by a foot, but his next arrow went straight through the fiend's armor and killed it. "Sweet!" he yelled, then felt an arrow pierce his hand.

"Lucky shot," Turner growled as Duff took him past, struggling to clear the underbrush.

Stormie and Frida had gotten hung up behind some rosebushes that their horses couldn't jump, but the thorny barrier offered some cover. They rained down arrows on the advancing line of skeletons, picking off several but receiving nonfatal hits themselves.

Poor Duff had backed himself and his rider into a corner of oak trees and mushrooms, with a knot of zombies coming their way. Turner jumped down and drew his iron sword, sending green zombie limbs flying in all directions. He could only slash so fast, though, and two of the zombies caught him with the wooden axes they carried.

Rob could still shoot, despite the pain in his hand. He and Saber twisted and turned through the trees and rode up to defend Turner.

"I'll cover you while you get back on Duff!" Rob shouted.

But he could not hold off the half-dozen skeletons, which had no difficulty leaping tangled brush to get within firing range.

Pa-twang! Three arrows lodged in Turner's chain-mail helmet.

"You call that cover?" he yelled.

Just then, a short, square-nosed griefer with three legs hopped up on a nearby mushroom and addressed them in a nasal voice. "We meet again, Turner!"

"Die, mutant!" Turner cried, sighting with his bow. He was too late. The griefer simply dropped down behind the mushroom and sent his skelemob forward.

The zombies that Turner had cut, but not killed, had spawned more of their foul kind. Now Rob fended them off with his sword. *But there are so many of them!* he thought, terror beginning to rise with the bile in his throat.

"Turner! Captain! Over here!" Frida called desperately.

She and Stormie had been surrounded by skeletons. Rob had to do something, fast!

He dropped his sword and put two fingers in his mouth, giving the loudest, longest whistle he'd ever produced, and then shouted, "Thing 1! Thing 2! Sic 'em!"

Their new wolf friend bounded down the mountainside to join its pack-mate. Snarling and slobbering, the two devoured Frida and Stormie's captors. Bones showered the ground, clanging like the world's worst xylophone.

Rob's stomach tightened, and he had to acknowledge that they were still outnumbered. "Battalion Zero! Retreat!" He checked his compatriots' stunned faces. "Don't wait! *Get out of here!*"

The wolves held off the mobs just long enough to allow the troopers to pick their way back toward the boundary with their mounts. Turner shifted in his saddle and called over his shoulder, "You're dead meat, Legs! You ain't seen the last of me!"

A volley of arrows followed his retreat, so Rob and Saber brought up the rear and skedaddled out of there in a hurry.

CHAPTER 11

ROB WAS RELIEVED TO FIND KIM AND JOOLS AT the ready when Battalion Zero came galloping back their way.

"Is anybody hurt?" Kim called.

"Nothing that won't keep!" Turner said, then added, "Let's head for the hills!"

The two wolves came bounding after them as they made for the mesa. Kim acted as lookout from her perch on Saber's rump, assuring them that no mobs were following them across the mountain ridge.

Safely back in camp, they each removed their armor, Turner ruefully poking his fingers through the damaged chainmail helmet. Jools offered the warriors plenty of cooked beef to restore their health after the hits they had taken from the skeletons' arrows. Rob wrapped his hand, and Kim swabbed some cuts on Armor's and Ocelot's forelegs caused by the sharp thorns of the rosebushes.

One by one, the soldiers gathered around the daylight campfire, and after seeing to the horses Kim joined them. "You guys took some heavy hits. What went wrong?"

What went wrong, indeed? Rob asked himself, anger replacing his fear. He tightened his fists at his sides. *Well, number one, I fell out of an airplane for no good reason and landed in the ocean in somebody else's world. Then I survived my first night, when I would've been better off dead.* He glanced at the battalion members, who sat in various stages of dejection. *Next I had to meet up with know-it-all Frida, and bigmouth Turner . . . and Jools, and Stormie, and Kim, who now turn out to be massively incompetent and worthless! What went wrong?*

"Everything!" he snapped. He lit into the group. "Frida, Stormie: Your intel sucks! Jools: Nice *plan*! Roofed forest was the one biome we *shouldn't* have attacked. And Turner . . ."

The sergeant at arms sat up defensively.

"You couldn't shoot your way out of a paper bag!"

"Now, wait a—"

"Kim," Rob continued, livid, "why didn't you prep our horses with potions of leaping? We were basically stonewalled."

"B-but . . . you never asked me to." Kim looked like she was about to cry.

"You're the master of horses." Rob stabbed a finger at her. "You're supposed to anticipate what they might need!"

Stormie said quietly, "Casting blame won't help us now, Captain."

"Get out of my sight!" he growled. When they sat there, stunned, he stomped off toward the abandoned mine shaft on his own.

Once inside, he took the steps two at a time, down to the bottom of the pit that reflected his state of mind. At the dead end, he took a left. He dropped a lit torch from his inventory on the dirt floor and, grabbing an old pickaxe, he began hacking away at the stone walls.

What good were masterminds and powerhouses if they could still make mistakes? He had trusted Jools to devise a failsafe battle plan. He thought Kim understood that their horses had to be able to jump an entire squadron of armored skeletons if they needed to. And he had counted on Turner, Frida, and Stormie to annihilate their attackers . . .

So I wouldn't have to, he confessed.

Shame stung his insides. What kind of a leader was he, anyway? Only a coward sends his troops up against an enemy that he won't face himself. Rob dropped his tool and slid to the ground in defeat.

After a moment or two, he lifted his head from his arms and stared at the wall. Then he noticed that the spot he had chopped away revealed something square and wooden inside.

Rob retrieved the pickaxe and enlarged the hole. He pulled and tugged, and soon a sizable chest popped out. Brushing away cobwebs and coal chunks, and a few iron ingots, he revealed an old, dusty book that was falling apart at the binding.

"What's this?" he said out loud.

As he pulled the book from the chest, a shiny glow rose from its surface.

This must be something important!

Forgetting his previous worries, he retraced his steps up the staircase and back to the center of camp. "Guys! Get a load of this!"

The others warily gathered around him, anticipating another tongue lashing.

Jools gave a start as he took in what Rob was holding. "Hand it over! That thing's powerful."

The rest watched as he turned the book over in his hands. "It's storing an enchantment!" he reported with excitement.

Turner pointed to their captain. "Let's test it out on him, then." He reached for the prize.

Jools jerked the book away. "Not a chance. This thing's good for one spell, and one spell only."

"Like what?" Frida asked.

"We could use it to beef up our armor," Stormie said knowingly.

"I got it!" Turner snapped his fingers. "We can use it to increase our take of loot. We could double or maybe even triple it!"

Jools held tightly to the book. "Or . . ." He grinned slyly and said, "We could use it to win our next battle."

*

The new strategy was brilliant, even Rob had to acknowledge that. It made use of their existing traps and would deal exponentially more damage to the griefer army via an enchantment of thorns.

"Normally, this spell works on armor to backfire on your attackers," Jools explained. "But I can tweak it to enhance our cactus traps!"

Rob considered this.

"That's all well and good," Turner complained, "but what do we use as bait?"

"Yeah. Those mobs are safely at the biome boundaries," Stormie reminded Jools. "How will we get them out here?"

Jools cocked his head. "Let me ask you this: What is it that skeletons love most?"

Turner put up a hand. "Killin'."

"That's right. And in the dark, they'll follow you through hell or high water to get within shooting range."

Kim realized what Jools was getting at. "We already know they're poor shots. They have to shoot ten times as many arrows as we do to strike a hit."

Frida picked up on the train of thought. "So . . . all we have to do is ride about fifteen blocks ahead of them and hope for the best."

Stormie nodded. "Leading them right into our traps!"

Rob clapped his hands. "It's a solid idea, Jools," he said, regretting his earlier tirade. "I'm sorry about what I said before. Everyone makes mistakes." He grinned at Jools. "Smart people learn from them."

Turner leaned closer. "And use them to kill dumb ones. I've got a score to settle with Legs, gang."

"Let's do it!" Stormie cried.

Rob wanted no more slipups regarding terrain. He should have known that a line of cavalry couldn't advance through a dense forest unimpeded. And once they were divided, they were easy targets. Jools, having ridden Beckett solo for so long, had overlooked that contingency. Rob used the error to remind his troops how important it was to act together.

They stepped up their horse drills to focus on alignment, and Rob made sure that Jools and even

Kim, whom he put up on Saber alone, could dress the line. Riders at either end checked with each other and sped up or slowed down if it was necessary to straighten everyone out. Then they could move as a unit.

Once they had acquired this skill, they had to apply it at every gait, and finally, over jumps. They would lure in the pursuing skeletons by jumping a camouflaged trap, leaving the mob to tumble in and die. There could be no wavering.

Their plan also required some extra scouting to locate the mob's nightly assembly point at a likely boundary. Stormie noted on the map that three borders came together at one spot adjoining the mesa. "If we could interest the mobs there, we could kill three giant, ugly birds with one deadly stone," she said.

"Skeleton mobs aren't exactly birds," Rob argued, "but I know what you mean. Three times the enemy troops, triple the damage. Great work, guys." He noted that a little praise went a long way with these individuals, and he vowed to lead them with more honey than vinegar from then on.

He charged Frida with mounting a nighttime mission to scout out the best place to attack, which she eagerly accepted. "Let me do it alone," she urged. "Stealth is my best weapon." Rob agreed, so Turner and Stormie stayed behind, working on ammunition and traps until she returned in the wee hours. When all was ready, they would head out at dusk.

The horses would be key to the success of their ploy. "Is there anything you want me to give them besides a potion of leaping?" Kim asked Rob the next day.

"Yes," Rob said, with a twinkle in his eye. His new method for motivating the enlisted players would sweeten the pot for the horses, too. "Give them sugar, Kim. Lots and lots of sugar."

*

Later that day, as the sun marched eastward and sky-blue deepened to violet overhead, the members of Battalion Zero double-checked their armaments. Although they planned a false retreat, they might have to resort to skirmishing.

"Turner, weapons report!" Rob commanded.

The sergeant at arms ticked off their increased inventory of bows and blades, augmented by a half-dozen iron pickaxes gleaned from the abandoned mine shaft. "They're old, but usable," he commented. He proudly presented maximum stacks of sixty-four newly crafted arrows to each trooper. "Retrieve 'em after a strike if you can!" he reminded them. "Otherwise the mobs will."

They did not expect to use the TNT cannon on this raid, as blowing off charges in their own camp seemed counterproductive. Turner deferred to Stormie and Kim, though, for the status of the cactus and suffocation traps. They had been mining, digging, and stacking in their spare moments until several booby traps had been rigged and then disguised. "Now, listen up!" Kim called. "You'll want to recall the *exact* location of these traps. They're meant for Dr. Dirt's monsters, not our precious horses. We've hidden them from view; these spots are for us to know and them to find."

Stormie had dyed swaths of wool with ore taken from the immediate area and stretched them over the pits. Now they looked just like the surrounding clay and sandstone, effectively shielding the traps from view. The battalion members walked off the locations on a grid lightly marked with sand and committed them to memory—except for Turner. Rob watched him write down the coordinates on the back of his hand. "Less I got to remember during a battle, the better," he said.

Jools listed the supplies they could count on in the thick of things or after taking one too many hits. There were elixirs to increase speed and strength, and potions of healing and regeneration. "I've got some extra helmets if you need one," he informed the group, "so come and see me before we leave if you do. And

Rob found some horse armor in that mine shaft chest. But that might interfere with your jumping."

They decided it would, and that they would trust the skeletons' bad aim and the interval they intended to put between them to keep Saber, Armor, Ocelot, and Duff safe. Kim had suggested penning the wolves, so they wouldn't be caught in the death traps while running down their prey.

"Good idea," Rob said.

Once again, there was nothing left for him to do before the battle but check in with his trusty steed. Saber was awake this time, having finished a light meal shortly before Rob arrived at the fence. No words or whinnies passed between the pair this time, only fervent wishes and heartfelt promises.

The four cavalry soldiers mounted up, leaving Kim and Jools to hold down the fort . . . and to welcome their enemies.

The riders journeyed to a high point where they could watch the intersecting boundaries yet remain hidden behind a dead bush screen. There, they dismounted and waited for the sun to set. Before long, they saw movement in the forest below.

It was just as Frida had scouted. As evening fell, ragged processions of zombies and skeletons, and a few chicken jockeys, marched and lurched toward the central border where the edges of the wooded forest, roofed forest, and desert connected to Bryce Mesa. If the enemy held the area, the three biomes opposite their mesa would essentially belong to Dr. Dirt and his legions.

"This ain't your land," Turner uttered through clenched teeth as they watched the mobs converge.

Rob gave the signal to mount. He summoned every bit of his courage and called, "Battalion Zero, by file: March!" Off went Stormie on Armor, followed by Frida on Ocelot. Rob and Saber followed Turner and Duff. *Who ever thought I would be riding voluntarily toward a pack of zombies and skeletons?* Rob thought.

Then one of the zombies noticed the horses' movements. The sentry quickly rallied more monsters, which groaned an alarm that sailed toward the intrepid cavalry. "Uuuuhhh, ooohhh, unnnhhh!"

"I dunno what they're saying," Turner mumbled, "but it ain't 'Happy Halloween'!"

Rob pressed his lips together. "Let's get this over with," he said. "Front into line . . . March!" The group picked up speed.

When they came within fifty blocks or so, they heard a shout from Legs, who sounded like he had a head cold: "Halt, intruders! These biome boundaries are the property of Dr. Dirt!"

Turner yelled back, "Only a weenie would do his dirty work for him!"

Battalion Zero continued their advance.

There was brief silence. Then Legs shrieked, *"Cha-a-a-rge!"*

Rob waited until the mobs were a dozen blocks away, and then instructed his riders: "Left wheel! And . . . forward!"

Like clockwork, the gang of four turned in sync, angling to the left until they formed a retreating line. Then they moved off as one, leading the bags of bones and staggering zombies away from the border.

"Faster, faster!" called Stormie, glancing over her shoulder at their pursuers and then down toward Rob to dress the line.

Arrows began to fall behind them.

"Don't bother to shoot back," Rob urged. "Just ride!"

The four horses, high on sugar and amped up on jumping potion, shot ahead.

"Slow down! Slow down!" Turner yelled. "Or they'll turn back."

It was a fine line to ride. They needed to bait the skelemob into giving chase without becoming human and equine pincushions that the trailing pack of zombies could fall upon and finish off.

"I'll get you yet, Turner!" shouted Legs in his stuffy voice from his safe position behind the mobs.

"Bring it on . . ." Turner muttered under his breath. "Bring it on!"

The many days of drilling and planning were about to pay off. The tiny battalion swept over the mesa in formation, leaving just enough ground behind them to entice the oncoming undead. They topped the low rise before their camp and thundered toward their secret target.

Turner needn't have wasted his time adding the pit coordinates to his tattoo collection. They were seared into Rob's brain. He'd have to give the others the command to jump at just the right time . . . or they would each die a prickly death.

The sound of horse hooves, jangling bones, unearthly groans, and gasping breaths filled the air. "Stormie!" called Rob. "Count down!"

She looked back to measure the shrinking buffer zone between the defenders and attackers. "Twelve blocks! Ten . . . nine . . . eight . . ."

The archers neared, but their aim grew worse.

". . . seven . . . six . . . five . . ."

Now the agitated zombies in their wake wailed louder.

". . . and . . . go!"

Rob prepared to give the order. "Jump, everyone! *Jump!*" In near-perfect timing, the four pairs of horses and riders communicated, responded, and leapt for the sky. Before they had even landed, waves of sprinting skeletons had permeated the wool-disguised cactus trap, cartwheeling in and being impaled by enchanted spines. It happened so fast that the second wave had no time to stop before gravity sent them forward, too.

The slower zombies, unable to detect even the most obvious danger, did not try to avoid the now visible pit. In they fell. Their griefer commander, however, recognized the decoy for what it was and jammed to a stop.

Legs frantically peered into the half-dark. His griefer reinforcements hadn't arrived yet. Spying a chicken jockey that was none too spry, he swiped the baby zombie rider's golden sword and knocked the green toddler into the pit. Then he jumped on the chicken's back, wheeled it around, and took off for the hills.

Turner prepared to send Duff after him, but Rob held out a hand. "Let him go," he said. "He can't hurt us without his mobs. And we need him to report our win to Dr. Dirt."

Kim and Jools released the stacks of sand into the churning pit, and by and by the creaking, wailing, and thumping ceased. It reminded Rob of the day he had killed the three zombies with his pillar of sand on the beach. That seemed so long ago now.

"All present and accounted for, sir!" Stormie reported. No one had taken an arrow. No horse had suffered a scratch.

"It doesn't get any better than this," Rob whispered to himself. Forgetting for a moment that this success was just the tip of the iceberg, the captain of Battalion Zero savored the knowledge that he had brought his troops through a battle victorious and unscathed.

CHAPTER 12

CELEBRATION KEPT THE BATTALION UP HALF THE night. Thing 1 and Thing 2 howled happily at the moon. Jools played DJ, amplifying disco music from his computer speaker. And who knew Frida could dance like that?

Meanwhile, Stormie inked up some unenchanted cactus needles and drew Turner a commemorative tattoo on a biceps he'd kept bare for just such an occasion. Kim and Rob spent time with the horses, just hanging out on the fence and tossing them chunks of carrot every now and then.

As the moon journeyed across the sky, everyone gravitated back to their customary spots around the campfire and replayed their conquest.

Turner was still pumped. "Did ya see the look on Legs's face when every last one of his skeletons fell for our trap?"

Jools reached over and shook his hand. "I liked watching him flee screaming on the back of a chicken."

Stormie turned to their leader. "So, what's next, Captain Rob?"

Turner cut in. "Let's just do this again!"

"I wish we could, Sergeant. I doubt it would work without the element of surprise, though."

Stormie moved closer to Rob. "Dr. Dirt will be onto us now," she agreed. "But I'm sure you and Jools will think of something."

Rob grunted. It was so easy to let her think well of him.

Frida grabbed an empty potion bottle and placed it on its side on the ground. "Let's let fate decide." She gave the bottle a spin. It came to rest pointing south, toward the extreme hills.

"Hill country!" she said. "I'll scout it out tomorrow."

"Hmm," Kim mused. "The zombies and skel-emobs would have to cross the desert to get there. You'd think they'd want to stay away from all that bright sun."

"That's where Dirt's plan actually makes sense," Turner reasoned. "His hostiles always have cover at least half the time. Night comes to every biome, generally around, well . . . sunset."

"Thank you for that succinct explanation, Sergeant," Rob said. "I've been studying the map. Those hills may be the key to unlocking Dr. Dirt's hold on the Overworld. I notice that they adjoin twice as many biomes as the forest we just liberated. Taking the extreme hills would bring peace to one-tenth of the entire mapped world." *And maybe buy me a ticket home.*

"World peace is an admirable goal," said Jools, "but necessity may require us to put the sunflower plains back on the drawing board, for now. If we don't rally there soon, the village and Kim's ranch might be lost."

Rob cast the horse master a quick look. She had said nothing about worry over the stock and property she'd left behind or the welfare of her villager friends. She had placed the good of the group above her own concerns. Perhaps they owed it to her to repay that loyalty.

"It's settled," Rob said. "We'll put the hills on the back burner for now. Frida, check into griefer activity on the western mesa boundary ASAP. We'll attack there, and then ride into the village to reinforce their dominion." He pictured the scene that they had left, smoke in the air and the iron golem's remains scattered across the ground. "Let's see if we can't give those folks back their freedom."

Kim skipped over and hugged Rob around the neck. "Oh, Captain! How can I ever thank you?"

He blushed, but said, "Maybe you can show me your vaulting technique sometime. . . ."

"Hey, y'all!" Stormie said. "I've got a surprise."

She hustled away from the campfire and called from a distance, "To victory!"

They saw a spark and heard a *whoosh*. Then the sky flowered with patterns of light—red, gold, green, purple.

Fireworks! Their artillery commander had secretly crafted them in her idle moments.

"Ooooh . . ."

"Ahhh . . ."

"Hoard the purple!" came the appreciative comments.

As the display popped off smaller charges and draped the sky with color, Stormie returned to stand beside Rob and watch. "That one's for you," she whispered, brushing against him.

It was as though she were a human magnet and he were a full suit of iron armor. But his role as commander meant that duty came first.

"Thank you very much, Artilleryman Stormie. Those were very thoughtful explosions." He turned on his heel, walked to the stream, and—gritting his teeth—jumped into the evening-chilled water.

*

Fresh from their conquest, Battalion Zero was well situated to mount an attack on the demons holding the plains/mesa boundary. Frida's undercover work revealed that Dr. Dirt and his legions had run rampant in the area, destroying every attempt by the plains villagers to rebuild their shattered town. Kim's ranch and horses were just a short ride away. Something had to be done.

Kim contacted Aswan on chat to hear his side of the story. "It's worse than we thought, guys," she told the war tribunal. "The griefers have taken all three plains boundaries and are basically holding the villagers captive in between. It's just a matter of time before they run out of supplies and manpower."

Rob knew she had to be consumed with worry for her horses, yet she focused on the villagers' plight. "There's no time to lose," he said to Jools. "I want your best-case and worst-case scenarios for attacking tomorrow night."

"Well, I've been working on it," the crafty quartermaster said. "Best case: We throw all the firepower we have at them first—cannon, flaming arrows, and a bunch of exploding creepers that I can generate using a spawn egg. While they're reeling from that, we hit them with archery fire from horseback and set Thing 1 and Thing 2 on them. Then, if anything is still standing, we mow them down with blades and axes on foot."

They all thought this sounded like a strong option.

"And worst case?"

"We run away," Jools said, shrugging his shoulders. "That's all I've got."

No one asked what the probability calculator predicted. If giving this battle their all wasn't enough, it wouldn't matter what the odds were.

This time, horse armor would be required. Unfortunately, none of the iron mesh pieces would fit Duff's massive chest or substantial derriere. Kim told Turner not to worry. "If any horse can take care of himself, it's Duff."

So when they assembled to set off for the biome border, Armor, Ocelot, Saber, and Beckett all matched their riders, decked out in protective gear, while Duff trotted along uncovered.

"I'm glad you didn't wear *your* birthday suit to complement your horse," Jools said to Turner. "Not that there's much bare skin on you anyway."

Turner leaned back in the saddle. "A man's got to have his tats," he said proudly.

The mood darkened along with the sky as they rode farther from camp and closer to the scene of their next battle. The two wolves' steady lopes even seemed subdued.

"I hope Aswan's all right," Kim said from the back of Rob's horse, where she was perched. "Turner, when I heard from him last, Aswan said Sundra had moved underground to escape the fires."

"That woman's resourceful," Turner replied. "Maybe I'll bring her back with me this time. We could use a good farrier."

Rob wasn't happy about leaving the broad mesa. This was not a life he would have chosen. *Nothing like long stretches of uneventful boredom, punctuated by terrifying warfare.* He allowed himself a brief thought of home with its soothing sounds of crickets and sage-scented breezes. That was what kept him fixed on defending a world in which he was a stranger . . . and an underdog.

Rob pushed the memory away and reviewed the strategy for the upcoming battle once more. If it did come down to hand-to-hand combat, "Battalion Zero" might be a more fitting description than he'd have liked.

*

Again, they used a brush screen to scan for the mob's appearance. Jools and Kim set up a supply station and Frida and Stormie snuck away to position the TNT cannon within range. They had to get in fairly close, so Jools agreed to move in after them with Ocelot, Armor, and the creeper spawn egg. Then he'd retreat with the girls once the creepers had spawned and were moving toward the enemy. Turner and Rob made ready to charge as soon as the first cannon shot wreaked damage.

At Rob's signal, the group went into action.

But someone was waiting for them.

Before Stormie could prime the cannon, a platoon of baby zombies wobbled toward her, arms outstretched. "Goooh-goooh, gaaah-guuuhhh!"

She fell back and called out to Rob, "What should I do, Captain?"

It was hard to believe that these awkward creatures meant them harm. The worst that could be said of them was that they smelled like rotting infants. When Rob hesitated, Turner yelled, "Blast 'em!"

Rob cut him a look, but echoed, "Blast 'em!" The slight delay enabled the quick-moving baby mob to reach Stormie and Frida, who were still on foot. The small monsters pulled their golden swords and initiated a melee. Tiny green limbs and heads flew everywhere while, behind them, a row of daddy zombies marched into position.

"Let's go, boys," Rob commanded Turner and Jools. Their horses responded to his voice and raced toward the girls, leaving Kim alone with the supply chest and the wolf guard.

"*Uuuuhh . . . ooohhh!*"

Rob and Turner held the zombies off with arrow after arrow, sometimes knocking off chunks of flesh and sometimes killing an attacker. The stench spread.

By the time Stormie was finally free to prime the cannon, Jools had formed his creeper mob and shown them across the battle line. "Send in the wolves!" he cried at Kim, and the two Things chased the creepers toward the enemy.

Stormie activated the TNT blast . . . but nothing happened.

No noise.

No explosion.

No bits of zombies raining down.

Rob eyed Turner. What could possibly have gone wrong this time?

*

"Puny . . . humans . . . of . . . Battalion . . . Zero!" came a high-pitched and well-enunciated address from the dark plains. "This biome . . . is *my own!*"

Stormie and Frida, who were collecting their horses from Jools, froze. Turner and Rob reined in Duff and Saber, unsure which direction to take.

Next came a rumbling so ominous, so deep, and so ground shaking that it could only be coming from beneath the earth.

"Have a taste . . . of . . . your . . . own medicine!" screamed Dr. Dirt. "And then . . . some . . . of . . . mine."

Horror dawning, Stormie realized what was happening and hopped in the saddle, motioning for Frida to do the same. "Go, go, *go!*" she ordered the others. "Back to our side of the border!"

"Retreat!" Rob cried, taking his own advice.

Just as they cleared the boundary, the earth seemed to split in two.

Ka-wooooom! A mighty detonation opened up a trench of soil, mortaring chunks of bedrock into the sky. Dr. Dirt had rerouted the TNT back at them, setting the very border ablaze.

Rob couldn't help but steal a glance over his shoulder as he led the riders back toward Kim's station. There, they regrouped and watched the plains boundary burn where it met the mesa.

"At least that oughtta keep them away from us," Turner said, gripping Duff's reins.

"Or not," Jools said gravely. He pointed. "Over there!"

Across the fire line came a cavalry unit of skeletons mounted on horses, leaping the deadly blaze as though they felt no pain.

"They're not turning back," Jools announced.

Kim screamed. "They're zombie horses!"

"We've got to get out of here," Rob said, transmitting his panic to Saber, who started bucking.

"Somebody help me with the supply chest," Kim called anxiously.

"Leave it!" said Jools, and he scooped her up onto the back of Beckett's saddle. "Now or never, Beckett. There's no time for potions."

The battalion lit out for their mesa camp followed by endless ranks of cavalry skeletons. The pursuers closed in on Rob and company, maintaining attack distance. Arrows flew thick enough that some hit their marks. First Kim, and then Frida and Stormie took painful hits. Duff suffered a flesh wound in his rump. Rob felt an arrow pierce his neck. And still the attackers came.

Rob scoured his memory for some bit of wisdom that would lead them to safety. Their horses' hooves were accustomed to the mesa hardpan and could keep this up for quite a ways. Zombie horses, though . . .

"Turner!" He steered Saber next to Duff. "What happens to zombies that lose their legs?"

Turner thought a moment. "They just keep going!"

"That's it. We'll run them into the ground. Battalion, gallop: March!"

"We're galloping as fast as we can, Captain!" Stormie cried.

"Don't stop!"

As they thundered over the rocky mesa, sure enough, the zombie horses behind them started to break up. A hoof here, a leg there, and gradually the distance between the two lines of soldiers widened.

When, at last, the skeletons could no longer maintain their firing range, they gave up and turned back for the plains.

"Holy mother of lapis lazuli!" Turner swore. "That was a close one."

They straggled into camp, hurt, frightened, and defeated.

Kim slid down from Beckett's rump. "Oh, no! Where are the wolves?"

They all gazed back at the burning battle line in the distance. Thing 1 and Thing 2 had been on the other side when their cannon had backfired. The wolves were lost, along with the fight.

Kim burst into pink tears.

Stormie moved over to comfort her. Frida confronted Rob. "Any more bright ideas, Captain?" she snapped. He had no reply.

Their health bars low, the bulk of their supplies left behind, the battalion had suffered more than a setback. They were crippled, and Dr. Dirt knew it.

Jools pleaded with his captain, "Let me and Stormie go to the Nether. We've been there before. We can find Colonel M and bring him here."

Rob reminded Jools that they had vowed to stay together and not split their ranks. "We can't afford to lose anyone or anything," he said miserably, knowing that he was more afraid than ever of descending below the Overworld. They would all have to do without Colonel M's help.

They drifted off to heal themselves, care for the horses, and rest by the cold campfire. As Stormie, Kim, Jools, Frida, and Rob gathered there, the absence of the tame wolves was noticeable and painful. But something else was missing. Rob looked around. Duff was out in the horse corral, but his rider was not.

"Has anybody seen Turner?" Rob asked.

They all eyed each other, not daring to answer.

*

Days passed, and the sergeant at arms did not return. They searched the old mine shaft and up and down the stream to no avail. Frida couldn't even locate any footprints. When last seen, Turner had been alive. And he'd left his horse behind. Where could he have gone?

Without one of his best combatants, Rob could not fathom how they would win the next battle, let alone a war for the Overworld. Now, more than ever, he needed real help.

To bolster their dwindling supplies, they walked out onto the mesa to pick up what the zombie horses and skelemob had dropped. Turner would never have approved of the skeletons' poorly fashioned arrows, but they were better than nothing. The hot sun intensified the reek of dead zombie parts, making the work nearly unbearable. Among the rotten flesh, odd bones, carrots, and potatoes, however, lay the most gruesome item of all. Frida held up a pink pony halter with diamonds set into the browband. "Anybody know whose this is?" she called to the others.

Kim approached, squinting, then ran the last few steps. "It's—it's mine! It belongs to Starla—" She broke off, visibly shaken. Slowly, she mouthed her conclusion: "Dr. Dirt has turned my horses into zombies."

This time Kim didn't cry. She seemed to gather every bit of her wisdom and strength and wind them about her waist like a belt that was holding her together. She gave Rob a silent, wordless plea.

He understood. This must be avenged. And they would not be able to do it on their own.

He stood, motionless, torn between action and caution. Then the knowledge of how he would feel if Saber were transformed by evil pushed him over the edge.

Never mind what he could and could not, would and would not, do. Help resided in the underworld, and that was where Rob would have to go. He couldn't just send Jools and Stormie. If he wanted to ask the utmost of his battalion, he would have to give that much of himself.

"Troops," Rob said, rising from the campfire and packing up his bedroll. "Make ready. All of you. We're going to the Nether."

CHAPTER 13

THE MEMBERS OF BATTALION ZERO PREPARED for their journey. Without a trip to the Nether, the fate of the Overworld, Kim's ranch, and Rob's return home would all be jeopardized. Jools's remaining supply chest contained enough obsidian, flint, and steel to create and activate one Nether portal, but not enough for two. So they would have to track their whereabouts while below ground and return to the entry site if they ever wanted to see the sun again—without having to die to do it.

Stormie's compass and map would be of no use to them. Borrowing a move from Turner's playbook, they each wrote down their Overworld camp coordinates on the backs of their hands. These should correspond proportionally to underworld numbers, but Jools reminded them that there were no guarantees.

"The light level and the foul terrain further muck up one's sense of direction down there," Jools said. "We'll have to leave a trail of bread crumbs."

"Huh?" Rob knew they didn't have any bread in their stores.

Jools said, "Colored mesa clay will do nicely as path markers once we're on the move. The first order of business, though, will be to wall in the portal and build a base shelter near it. That way, if something does happen to the portal, we'll have somewhere to hole up."

Rob gulped. The thought of not being able to get back here felt too much like not being able to get back home . . . and only one other thing was worse than that. "I understand that in the Nether there's a higher probability of . . . death. What then?"

"You'll respawn up here," Stormie answered. "Then just use your flint and steel to reactivate the portal and rejoin us. So, if anyone goes missing, the rest of the battalion will rendezvous at our temporary base."

"But that can severely slow us down," Jools pointed out. "So, don't."

"Don't die?" Rob sat up straight. "Not if I can help it. But how about hunger?"

"With all the fires and fire starters, at least we won't have to worry about cooking meat," Frida said with a wry grin. "Wish we had some marshmallows."

Rob imagined himself as a human marshmallow skewered on a stick and roasting over a flaming lava pit. He could hardly wait. *Not.*

Aside from taking food and defensive supplies, there wasn't much more they could do to prepare themselves. The question was what to do with the horses.

"We can't ride them through the portal," Jools explained. "It simply won't work. We can, however, lead them through."

Rob wondered how well they would like that.

"You're projecting your thoughts on them," Kim reminded him. "Forget what you know about the underworld. Think like a horse. They don't know they're going to the Nether. They don't anticipate. They only know they're going where you ask them to go, and that they trust you."

"So . . . just walk right through confidently, then?" Rob offered.

Kim gave a shadow of a smile. "And bring lots of treats!"

They filled their inventories with sugar, carrots, weapons, and ammunition, leaving items for crafting torches and brewing potions in their stash at camp. Glowstone would serve as a passable light source below, and Jools could set up an alchemy station in the Nether, if necessary, where ingredients for base potions were plentiful.

Rob wished he had apprenticed with Turner in crafting arrows, though. The ones he made were nearly as clumsy as the skeletons' ammo. Stormie and Frida added better ones to the stacks, while Kim concentrated on filling their cobblestone, wood, and iron inventories. They would find none of those shelter-building resources in the land of netherrack and fire.

Compromised though his command seemed to be, Rob took stock of the situation as best he could. Addressing the four troopers, he said, "The horses will be our best assets on this mission. We'll be able to move faster than on foot or teleporting. So, Kim, except for going through the portal, I want you mounted on Duff."

She nodded silently. The missing rider on everyone's mind went unmentioned.

Rob turned to Jools. "Quartermaster, since you're the only one of us who has had direct contact with Colonel M, you'll be our liaison. We'll need your active participation in this assignment." He paused. "Will we have it?"

"Unquestionably," Jools replied.

"Right on," Stormie said, approving of the more equal battalion footing. "I volunteer to mark our way. Even without the map and compass, if one person keeps track, we'll have a better chance of staying on course. Less arguments."

"*No* arguments," Rob insisted. "We must act as a unit. The world depends on it."

They donned their armor and plied the horses with treats. At last, there was nothing more to it but to be on their way. The portal was built, the fire activated, and their hellish subway gaped open, waiting.

One by one, they led their horses through—first Stormie and Armor, then Frida and Ocelot, Kim and Duff, and Jools and Beckett. Their captain took one more look at the sunshine, chirruped to Saber, and walked into the portal block. Purple light diffused and reformed around them. The sounds of a thousand whimpering children swirled about the space.

Once again, Rob entered the unknown. His panic triggered an all-too-real memory of his initial freefall from the airplane and plunge into the ocean. Were it not for Saber at the end of his lead rope, he would have screamed until it killed him, he was sure. But a man had to lead a horse, or the horse would end up leading the man—and not always where he wanted to go.

All of the riders had learned this lesson the hard way during training. They steeled themselves, which was less of a stretch for survivalists Frida and Stormie, and in a few moments each reanimated in the lower dimension. Kim had been right; the horses followed them right through and onto sharp netherrack, which their shod hooves handled nicely.

They moved forward by file. The air smelled of sulfur and carbon, and left a dank residue on exposed skin. Rob's eyes adjusted to the gloom just in time for him to avoid stepping off a narrow ledge and into a broad lake of shimmering lava.

"I'll find us a clearing where we can mount," Stormie whispered from her place up front. "It's impossible to try to fortify the portal with stone from here. We can barely move on this ledge."

The high netherrack cliff on one side and the deep-looking lava pool on the other made Rob dizzy. He quietly reached forward and grabbed Beckett's tail, trusting the sure-footed beast to lead him onward. Suddenly, a blaze erupted just behind Saber, who was bringing up the rear. Feeling flames near his bottom, the horse jumped forward, bumping hard into Rob, who kissed Beckett's behind and created a chain reaction.

"Hey!"

"Oof!"

"Oww!"

"What th—?"

Fortunately, their motion was forward, not sideways and down.

"Sorry, guys!" called Rob. "I didn't have time to practice ring-of-fire exercises with Saber." In fact, his horse was noticeably spooked and scrabbled along the precarious netherrack ledge until Stormie found a side trail that led to a clearing. Here, they stopped and got their bearings, such as they were.

Rob sensed that as long as they remained somewhat calm, their horses would, too. He fought off fears of all the wicked mobs he had heard about and started giving orders in what he hoped was his normal voice. "Frida, Ocelot should be able to navigate these weird trenches pretty well. Scout the immediate area for a base site."

"Yes, sir!" She rode off warily.

"Stormie, Kim. Put your heads together to choose the quickest route to the Nether fortress we're looking for. Jools, you'll determine a way around obstacles that will keep us alive until we get there."

"How are you doing, Captain?" Stormie asked, concerned.

"I'm all right," Rob said, thinking, *I'm scared spitless.* "I'll keep a lookout," he promised, thinking, *For all the good that will do.*

It was fortunate that he could be at least marginally useful as a sentry, because all Rob could manage to do was goggle at his surroundings. He had never been so awestruck, had never laid eyes on anything like this place. The completely unfamiliar landscape reminded him of the time he had eaten a horny toad. A friend had killed and grilled the lizard while they were camping together once, and Rob remembered the sensation of putting something in his gullet that had never before entered his system. He had worried for a moment that he might turn into a spiky reptile, himself. Nothing happened, of course, but he couldn't help thinking that, from that moment on, he was a different person. Even if by a molecule.

What does that make me now? he wondered, surveying his surroundings. This dimension appeared to be sandwiched between bedrock, with glowstone light from overhead blocks, though not quite enough to actually see—he had to make out the outlines and imagine the rest. The area adjacent to the lava lake was brighter, but there was nothing really recognizable except a few desiccated trees. The formations that rose from the ground might have been crafted by a sloppy giant that chewed up netherrack and vomited it all over the place. Some blocks were broken by sharp crevasses, while others were whole and burned endlessly.

This dark and strange underworld, Rob feared, would become lodged so deeply in his soul that nothing would ever be the same again.

*

They heard snorting, and Rob made out a group of squat, pink and green zombie forms. "Pigmen!" he whispered, and Jools waved his hands silently, indicating that nonaction was best.

"Ignore them," he advised. "Treat them like Endermen, and they won't bother us."

So Rob fought off the instinct to attack the mutant zombies with his iron sword. He jiggled the lead rope a little to take Saber's attention off of them. When they had passed by and Frida returned, the rest of the riders mounted and followed her a short distance to a relatively flat area that was wide enough to hold a small shelter.

Kim held the horses and sang to them a bit while the others set to forming cobblestone walls and a roof and crafting iron bars for the windows. "I hate using a wooden door," Frida said, placing it last, "but it'll have to do for now."

Stormie crafted a few reddish-orange clay pillars to mark the spot. "If you get separated or if you die and respawn, find your way back to this spot. The rest of us will meet you here," she said. The group left some spare supplies there in a chest.

They moved off in the direction Jools had figured out would lead them to the fortress where Aswan said they could find Colonel M. Stormie's sensible horse, Armor, was certainly the right choice to lead the group. Ocelot, Beckett, and even Duff had broken a nervous sweat, compounded by the warmth of the bubbling lava lake that they were skirting. Rob held Saber back a few more lengths than usual because he kept wanting to bolt forward, and starting a stampede was out of the question.

Rob's resolution to remain calm was soon undone. In the eerie silence, a squeaking arose like a screen door on a rusty hinge. A string of babyish moans followed, but Rob saw nothing. As the battalion veered away from the burning lake, though, a huge, hovering cube swooped down on them.

"Ghast!" yelled Jools.

The colossal, bulky creature floated much more smoothly than Rob thought it should have. Its top-heavy cube was offset by half a dozen wriggling legs, like a badly drawn jellyfish. *How dangerous could that be?*

As if in answer, the ghast loosed a massive fireball at them, then two more. *Toom! Toom, toom!* The bombs all landed nearby, splitting the netherrack apart and causing the horses to buck and everyone to hold on for dear life. No wonder the terrain was so messed up, Rob thought, pulling Saber's head around so he would stop crowhopping. These ghasts either couldn't see or couldn't aim, or both.

The hovering ghast chortled and launched another fiery rocket. Frida and Stormie shot useless arrows at the blob, but Jools had the presence of mind to wait until the fireball came into range. As Rob and Kim watched, he punched at the thing. Instead of exploding, it ricocheted back at the ghast. *Whoom!* One ex-ghast.

They cheered, and Jools ducked his head modestly. "I was quite the batsman in cricket," he said.

Frida went to retrieve the gunpowder and ghast tear that dropped when the mobster exploded. "Go ahead!" she called. "I'll catch up."

They had to keep moving at all costs. Their health and hunger would be much more difficult to manage down here, and the sooner they found the colonel, the sooner they could leave.

They followed a largely diagonal path, sidestepping pits, trenches, and small lava pools. But when they came to a burning stream that rushed off the side of another cliff, they realized they'd have to cross it. The less experienced riders were not thrilled.

Rob muscled Saber up to the bank. "Let me go first," he urged. "Follow my lead. Keep your speed up, and for goodness sake, don't look down!" If he could trust Saber to do one thing well, it was to jump almost anything. But a flaming ribbon of molten lava?

Rob clapped his heels against Saber's sides and did his job as rider—*thinking* them over the fence, centering himself above Saber's own balancing point, and, most importantly, not looking down. That was all the horse needed. If only Rob could have watched the pair of them, hurdling the burning barrier as though it were just another jump in a steeplechase. When Saber's front feet hit netherrack, Rob called over his shoulder, "Battalion, charge! *Jump!*"

He didn't dare turn around, or the other horses might falter. He reined Saber to a stop and waited. Armor arrived, puffing; Ocelot pulled up, nostrils flared; Duff thundered up, barely winded. . . .

"Team!" came Jools's plaintive voice from behind.

They had to look. Beckett danced on the other side, refusing to leap the fiery river.

There was nothing for it—Rob whirled Saber around and repeated their performance back to the other side. Then he tossed Jools one end of a lead rope. "Kick him!" he ordered, and both mounts took off at a nervy gallop, Saber ponying the stouter horse along. "Again!" Rob cried, and with a desperate nudge Saber launched, followed by Beckett, landing neatly on the other bank.

"Now, pet him," said Rob, doing the same to Saber with a shaky hand. Horses were amazing animals. Certainly more amazing than humans.

Kim distributed sugar blocks for all.

They continued on the path that Jools had worked out, with Stormie placing clay markers as they went. Suddenly, she halted Armor and scratched her helmeted head. Here were clay pillars of the same color in front of them. They walked a bit farther and found another . . . and another.

Was someone trying to disorient the battalion? Had another party coincidentally laid the same trail markers?

Rounding a bend in a netherrack wall, an immense, dark structure towered before them made entirely of bricks, with a pile of reddish-orange clay blocks in front of it. From within, they could hear the rattle of brittle bones and the crackle of fire. Smoke hung in a dead cloud around the edifice. A sliver of torchlight appeared as the brick gate swung open.

Somebody was home.

CHAPTER 14

"I'VE BEEN WAITING FOR YOU," CAME A DEEP MALE voice that was both hollow and rich, like a solemn drum beat.

The riders held their breath as the gate swung wider.

The space filled with a huge human face, with skin like well-worn Havana leather, eyes brighter and sharper than ghast fireballs, and wild silver hair that stood on end in some places and flopped over in others. Behind the powerful stare was a measure of humor that Rob was thankful to see. It was the most approachable looking gigantic head he had ever encountered—and, of course, the only one.

Oddly, he could see right through the facial features to a row of torches burning high on an iron grid and something writhing in the half-light behind it. Rob elbowed Jools.

"Y-yes, right," Jools stuttered, flustered for once. He pressed the reluctant Beckett forward. "Colonel M? We met awhile back."

"I remember you," thundered the head, causing the rest of the horses to sidle back a few steps. "You played a small role in helping my friends liberate their redstone generator from the hands of the syndicate."

"Well, I—"

"And now you want me to return the favor."

"Not that you owe me . . ."

". . . anything. Then why do you seek me?"

Jools looked at Rob. "Well, we—"

The head cut him off. "I know why you have come. Why are you not riding these horses against your enemies in the Overworld instead of wasting time at my door? I do not take kindly to solicitors."

This made Rob angry. "We're not selling Girl Scout cookies, *sir*," he said, with a touch too much emphasis.

The head's mouth opened as wide as the gate. "Silence!" it boomed, causing horses and humans to quake. "You have no right to request aught of me without payment of some sort." The colonel's head waited. *"Well?"*

Kim pressed a reluctant Duff up to the gate. From her inventory she took the pink pony halter that had belonged to one of her stolen herd. "For your horse, sir." She cleared her throat. "It's adjustable."

"Well, perhaps the diamonds could be of some use. . . ." the head murmured, punching every other word like a bass drum.

The gate swung wide and the head dipped in luke-warm welcome.

There the riders dismounted and led their skittish horses into the fortress vestibule. Rob could make out a large, brick room with an iron grate for a back wall, which held back the rattling, jittery creatures that pounded against it from the other side. They resembled the skeleton mobs he'd fought off before, but they were as black as coal and held stone swords instead of bows. The swords made a jackhammer racket, clattering in and out of the iron crosshatching.

"Wither skeletons," Jools commented. "Nice guard dogs."

"They do my bidding," Colonel M said as his head floated backward to make space for the players and their horses.

"Nice of you to set up this skeleproof room," Stormie said, trying to break the ice.

"For approved visitors only," the colonel stated, eyes flashing.

In the additional brightness, Rob saw something move in a corner of the entrance hall. He turned and, startled, fell against Saber's shoulder.

"About time you got here," came a familiar gruff voice.

There sat Turner, intact and alive, with his feet casually propped up on a small magma cube. The black footrest radiated heat from its red, yellow, and orange eyes.

As the group recognized him and stared, he said, "I was just telling the colonel here about forcing old Legs to retreat on chickenback."

Colonel M huffed a chuckle. "Wise move, those pit traps," he acknowledged, then cocked his head at Rob. "Is this the innocent you mentioned?"

"Newbie, yeah. Colonel M, meet Captain Rob. Newbie . . ."

The ghostly head sized up Rob and his horse. "Ender Dragon fodder," he spat. "But you may rest here briefly. Then be on your way."

"Turner!" Frida exclaimed. She frowned. "How is it that *you're* here?"

"I didn't think Captain Newbie would survive a trip down under. I dismantled my portal once I crossed over so he wouldn't fall in and die."

Rob saw red. "Thanks, Turner, but I can take care of myself. What you've done is high treason." The stunt had cost him and Frida, Kim, Jools, and Stormie hours of worry and worthless searching.

"Treason!" the colonel repeated. "How so?"

"If you please, sir," Rob began, "our cavalry unit was preparing to defend the Overworld against a griefer boundary takeover. Turner here went AWOL."

The colonel's eyes darkened. To Turner, he demanded, "Explain yourself, soldier!"

"Yes, do," Frida said, tight-lipped.

Turner pushed the subdued magma cube away and leaned forward. "Found the fortress coordinates in Kim's browser history. Thought I'd offer my services to the colonel before pestering him with our . . . little problem."

"Little problem!" Stormie echoed. "If you call a world war *little*—"

Colonel M's gaze flashed between the two like a searchlight.

"Well, to him, mebbe it is little," Turner defended himself. "In fact, he thought he could use some paid muscle to keep the mobs in line. We was just getting down to the nitty-gritty when you showed up."

Jools was upset about the danger Turner had put them all in for personal gain. "You're saying that you'd prefer to stay here if you got a better offer?"

The mercenary relaxed and put his feet back up. "I know there ain't as many savory women in the Nether, but for the right salary, a guy could live here quite comfortably. . . ."

The head seemed to grow as it drew itself as upright as a disembodied skull could. "Money," said Colonel M, "has no place in a just quest." His eyes shot a beam that knocked the magma cube out from under Turner's feet, causing the sergeant to lurch forward and fall to the ground. "My offer is withdrawn. Now go, all of you. Before I open the interior gate!" He flew threateningly over to the torch-lit grid, through which the wither skeletons poked their swords and bony arms.

The horses strained at their handlers, terrified. Turner and the others scrambled toward the fortress entrance—except for Rob. "No," he said, gripping Saber's reins with all his might.

Colonel M could scarcely believe his eyes. This tiny dragon bait of a man? Defying him?

Rob had not come all this way to be slapped aside like an annoying insect. Again, his terrifying first night came back to him, and all the trials he'd faced. Losing Turner, and Kim's horses, and having to bring his friends to the most awful, dangerous place on the map . . . He had put himself on the line and had nothing but pain to show for it.

"You were supposed to be this great legend," Rob snapped at the gargantuan ghost. "This cavalry expert who could do no wrong." He let go of Saber's reins and approached the colonel, letting the horse back away toward the others. "Look at you! You don't even have a body. The only forces you're commanding are a bunch of burned-up skeletons. The only 'just quest' you're interested in is one that'll keep people in need from knocking on your door. If you don't care about us," he said, waving at his compatriots, "you could at least give our horses some shelter. They worked their butts off getting us here . . . and they're afraid!"

The entire assemblage was stunned into silence. Their host's patience had nearly come to an end, and a swift death for all might certainly be coming.

Rob quoted, "'In no case should a horse be punished for timidity.'"

The colonel's terrifying glare broke. "*Cooke's Cavalry Tactics*, 1862," he murmured. "A good cavalryman puts his horse first." A ray of amusement returned to his eyes. "I like your style, Captain. And I thank you for the reminder." He nodded at Rob. "It has been quite some time since I commanded horse soldiers."

"I don't suppose you have any water," Rob muttered. "They could use a drink."

*

Colonel M's ghostly state required no water, or food, for that matter, but his horse, Nightwind, was still in bodily form. The officer invited his visitors to help themselves from his fireproof storage of hay and his infinite water source.

"He must have some ace powers to keep water here in the Nether," Jools said, watching Beckett slurp from a bucket.

"How else d'you think he gets by with just a head?" Turner said.

"I'd sure like to know how he ended up this way," Stormie whispered.

Their host floated toward them from a back room. "I'll tell you how it happened," he boomed. "In the final battle of the First War, my unit was far outranked by the unified hostiles. My men needed a decoy to allow them to double back and surround the enemy from its rear flank."

"You!" Rob gasped.

The head nodded. "Me. I took so much damage all at once that I could never respawn with my body."

"But . . . what about Nightwind?" Kim asked.

"I'd left him ground tied, out of range. He never budged an inch."

"Awesome training," she said, appreciating his skill.

"But why did you move to the Nether?" Frida wanted to know.

Colonel M regarded her with a bemused expression. "It seemed like a good idea at the time." He bobbed down the line of horses, checking to see that they'd drunk from their buckets and were finding the hay palatable. "And now seems like a good time to return to the Overworld. Try to finish what I started."

"You mean—you'll help us?" Rob blurted out.

The disembodied colonel nodded at the rest of the battalion. "You have everything you need right here," he said. "What I can do is provide supervision."

Rob had never been so thrilled by the thought of someone telling him what to do. But he had to maintain his authority. "We'd be proud to have you ride with us, Colonel. But I command this unit."

Again came the bemused expression. "That is not a job I wish to reclaim. I'm a civilian now. A colonel in name only."

Their counsel secured, all the battalion had to do now was backtrack to their portal.

"Nothing like a quick trip to the Nether, I always say," Turner commented from his perch on Duff.

Colonel M had entrusted Nightwind to Kim, after hearing her history and watching how quickly she charmed the horse. Nightwind was the tallest animal she had ever ridden, yet his body was so well-rounded that he didn't seem overlarge from the saddle. He responded to the slightest shift of her small pink frame, so effectively, in fact, that she didn't need to do anything with the reins but hold them steady.

The pair led the rest of the group without incident over the lava stream where Beckett had balked. They picked their way back along the trail of clay pillars left by Stormie. She mentioned to Turner how his markers had tipped them off that something was up.

"Great minds think alike," he said, causing Colonel M to roll his massive eyes at Rob.

Fear sprouted, however, when a numerous mob of wither skeletons blocked their path on the narrow ledge that rimmed the lava lake. Thanks to Colonel M's presence, though, the threat never took hold. Those that yielded to his command to stand down literally withered in his presence; those that placed arrows to blackened bows were summarily blown by the colonel's oversized lips into the molten sea, where they shrieked, burned, and sank dead away.

As the party climbed closer to the portal through which they had entered the Nether, Stormie questioned their orientation.

"It was—right here," she stammered.

Now it wasn't.

With some squinting and crouching over the ledge's edge, Frida identified a partial section of obsidian block stuck in the netherrack cliff like a cookie in an ice cream sundae. "Looks like this is all that's left of it!" she cried. "Must've been destroyed by that ghast. Let's head for the shelter and craft a new portal there."

Turner's reclaimed obsidian would be enough to construct it. While he and the others got to work crafting, Rob felt an overwhelming drowsiness wash over him. This leadership business took a lot out of a fellow. With everything under control, perhaps he could afford to take a short catnap. He pulled his bedroll off the saddle and left Saber with the other horses.

Frida glimpsed him heading for the stone shelter. "What're you—?"

He ducked inside, squatted on the floor, and unrolled the woolen bed.

Frida sprang for the door. "Rob! Don't do that!"

"Don't do what?" he asked climbing into the sleeping bag and preparing to get some shut-eye.

Foom! The sudden explosion was strong enough to throw the vanguard backward, into the branches of a dead-leaved tree.

*

I'll never live this one down, Rob thought as Jools and Stormie carried his limp body to the new Nether portal. Worse, his health bar had taken a nosedive.

"How many times have I got to tell you?" Turner upbraided the captain. "Never go to sleep in the Nether!"

"You didn't tell me," Rob grumbled. "And how was I supposed to know that my bed would blow up!"

Frida winced. She had taken pride in keeping her naive friend safe thus far. She, too, had received some damage from being hurled at the tree and then falling onto sharp, uneven netherrack. After Turner activated the portal and waved Jools, Stormie, and Rob through, he let Frida lean on him, and they entered the purple mist once more.

Kim led Armor, Saber, and Ocelot through the dimensional pathway.

Colonel M drifted behind Beckett, Duff, and Nightwind, guiding them through. The freshly augmented Battalion Zero moved back into the sun and trudged wearily toward their camp.

Smoke rose in the distance. Stormie put a hand up, halting their progress. For a brief moment, she wondered if the portal had failed. Dozens of small fires burned where their base camp should be. Were they still stuck in the Nether?

But the sun shone, and the mesa was otherwise as they had left it. They wandered into camp. The only sign of life was a very large chicken, which bobbled around in circles.

"Griefers!" Jools muttered.

"One griefer in particular," growled Turner. "That there chicken's a sign from Legs." He threw Duff's reins to Kim, stalked over, and pushed the demented bird into one of the fires. He picked up the cooked meat that was dropped and passed it around the group. "That *there's* a sign from me," he said, more bent on revenge than ever now.

But retaliation would have to wait. "We're as helpless as ocelot kittens!" Jools told the group. "We just lost a supply chest in the Nether shelter, and now our communal stores have been plundered."

How would they mount an attack with no armor, potions, weapons, or ammunition?

"I told you consolidating our inventories was stupid," Turner complained to the captain, who lay still next to their old campfire pit. It, too, had been set on fire.

Rob didn't have the strength to impose sanctions on the sergeant for insubordination. But he did throw a bucket from his personal inventory at him and told him to go put the fires out.

*

Thanks to a potion of regeneration that Jools and Colonel M worked up, health and vigor gradually returned to Battalion Zero's leader. His dignity, though, had taken a more permanent beating. He couldn't help feeling that the loss of supplies was his fault. The mistake might cost the team everything they had hoped to accomplish.

As he walked along the mesa stream thinking, Colonel M joined him. Having been in Rob's shoes before, he understood his dilemma clearly. The old ghost asked the newbie commander, "What is it that makes a cavalry a cavalry?"

"Well . . . horses," answered Rob. "And men," he added, and the colonel nodded.

"In some cases," Colonel M said, "whole battles have been fought without a single blade. Consider your effective traps." They walked a bit farther. "Now you can't repeat a successful strategy . . . but you *can* modify it."

The two discussed how they might use subterfuge to enable them to get back to the village, resupply, and regroup for another assault on Dr. Dirt. "You're thinking too much about modern warfare," Colonel M pointed out. "How can you use the two things you've got to get what you want?"

Horses . . . and men. Rob envisioned them as chess pieces and moved them around in his mind. The horses, including Beckett if he had a strong lead, would carry them through a charge at the village or any other battle line. *What does everyone else do best?* Rob asked himself, thinking of his players. They were a very talented group. If he capitalized on their strengths, they could win without firing a shot.

There was no sense in sticking around the ruined campsite. Rob called the battalion together. "Kim! We need some intel from Aswan. Find out if the town replaced their iron golem. And Turner, see if Sundra has enough metal to arm the villagers with good shovels."

Turner looked at him sideways.

"No smart remarks, now. Jools, Stormie, let's study that map again."

Colonel M stood back, satisfaction blanketing his face. "That boy's a born leader," he remarked to Frida, who surprised herself by agreeing with him. It hadn't been so long ago that she had been able to trick Rob with a wooden carrot. He had come a long way.

Kim reported that the village did have a new iron golem, and Turner had cajoled Sundra into crafting as many sturdy shovels as she could.

"Now what?" Stormie asked. She had located a rise behind the village that could be connected to the top of the outer wall by a bridge, essentially forming a back door where one did not yet exist. Such a breach would leave the village vulnerable—*if* an enemy knew about it.

Jools snapped his fingers, making all sorts of connections. "We get Aswan and friends to install this bridge during the day, when Dirt's legions are off in their caves. They camouflage it . . ."

". . . using dyes and wool to paint the normal wall scene on a facade," Stormie offered. "No one will be the wiser."

"Then Aswan relays the order to dig a moat at the front gate, where Dirt always strikes," Jools continued. "Ditto with the camouflaging."

Now Frida could see where the plan was heading. "The iron golem stays on the village side of the moat, and the skeleton and zombie mobs will rush to assault it, to get at the villagers." She paused. "But what sets off the mobs? How do we know they'll show?"

Rob grinned. "We set up a network chat from a bogus source, saying that a huge shipment of gems has been delivered to the village. Dr. Dirt can't resist an easy score."

Jools nodded. "While all of that transpires, we'll have ridden in through the back door, and we'll hold the fort until sunup."

Now the outcome dawned on Turner. "Every last monster in the moat will burn to a crisp."

Kim clapped her hands. "And we'll get the supplies we need, with no one standing in our way between the village and my ranch!"

Rob hoped they would have some good news when they got there. Retreating to the ranch would allow them to attend to their horses, whose feet desperately needed new shoes after traversing netherrack.

Sometimes you have to backtrack in order to make progress, he thought.

Colonel M read his mind. "Now you've got it, Captain," he said with a twinkle in his extremely large eyes. "A good strategist can't think in just one direction."

"Hear, hear," said Jools.

Turner scowled. "That Legs is gonna find that out. What goes around comes around."

CHAPTER 15

F RIDA'S SUGARCANE HAD BEEN TORCHED, AND KIM was fresh out of carrots and hay for the horses. Before they struck camp, Rob sent the two girls north and east to gather grass and apples for their stores. Turner and Stormie were put to work in the old mine shaft to replenish their iron, gold, and gemstones so they could trade in the village and work on armaments after they reached the ranch. They also placed the old mine carts they found in the battalion inventory.

Colonel M graciously offered to share his larder of brewing ingredients. He and Jools went into a huddle and cooked up the base potions they would need to help safeguard the village. Then, their tasks fulfilled, Battalion Zero said good-bye to the mesa hideout and headed for the plains border.

As they rode along with the colonel's head gliding beside them, the group filled him in on the action they had seen together.

"You made your entrance in the wake of Lady Craven's exit?" Colonel M said to Stormie, obviously impressed. "A genius with artillery is behind many a grand triumph."

"But we lost the TNT cannon at the plains battle," Stormie confessed with regret.

"I didn't want to turn tail. . . ." Turner said, trying to preserve his reputation.

"That's funny," Jools mentioned. "I recall Duff withdrawing at the head of the line with a skeleton arrow sticking out of his butt."

"Horse has got a mind of his own," Turner griped.

"At least he's still a real horse," Kim said tearfully, thinking of her mutated herd.

Rob described their pursuit by Dr. Dirt's mob mounted on zombie horses and their fears that he had transformed all of the stock Kim had spent years breeding on the ranch.

The corners of the giant mouth turned downward. "Such dirty tactics," the colonel remarked, deeply affected by the loss of so many good horses. "That griefer lives up to his name. And suggests a final resting place where we might send him."

This show of solidarity bolstered Rob's spirits. After feeling alone and broken for so many days, hope seeped back into his mind and body. *Wars aren't won with brute strength alone,* he thought, although he had to admit that having Turner at his back would be a real asset . . . if the mercenary were dependable.

They discussed their short-term plans. Assuming the ruse with the moat worked to diminish Dr. Dirt's ranks, they would be able to safely make a run for the ranch. A brief hiatus there would prepare them to advance on the extreme hills—and perhaps break Dirt's hold on it and the six surrounding biomes.

"A key target if ever there was one," Colonel M agreed. "But those hills . . ." He shuddered, causing him to bump into—and pass through—Ocelot, who kept going as though nothing had happened.

"I reckon she's ghost broke, now!" Frida said proudly.

"What about those hills, Colonel?" Rob persisted.

The transparent man said nothing for a moment. "The extreme hills are not to be trifled with," he finally replied. "They are treacherous. They offer little cover but many junctures for ambush. They are—" He hesitated. "—they are where I lost myself."

Rob felt an avalanche tumble toward the pit of his stomach. "The extreme hills? *That's* where the final battle of the First War took place?"

Turner cast him a glance. "Thought you knew that."

Now Rob eyed Frida. She had said nothing of this when they first talked about a vantage point and how it might help him get back home.

Frida ducked her chin. There had been no sense in stating the ominous truth back when they had met. Rob had needed something to cling to, not the likelihood that he would never find a way out of this world.

Now the implications of this news hit the erstwhile cowboy hard.

He implored his mentor, "Are you saying that the site is indefensible?"

The colonel chose his words carefully. "I'm not telling you that an attack there is impossible. It all depends on what you truly hope to gain by it."

Could they defeat Dr. Dirt's army? Would taking the extreme hills spell the beginning of the end for the evil griefer's conquest of the Overworld—or for Battalion Zero? More importantly, would Rob discover a window into his old life there?

There was only one way to find out.

*

The villagers made ready as Kim and Turner had requested. Aswan waved enthusiastically from the drawbridge the townspeople had built to connect with the hillside. The riders could see his neat, white apron from quite a ways off. With the optical illusion the paint job had created, it looked as though someone were waving a flag of truce from midair.

"Kim, my sweet dream!" called Aswan as they approached. "Your wish is my command."

She ignored his compliment as usual but expressed pleasure at seeing him again. They crossed the bridge, which he secured behind them, and entered the walled town.

"What a fine steed you ride," he observed. "A match for your beauty!"

Frida and Stormie jostled each other.

"And you two aren't so bad yourselves. . . ." Aswan reflected.

Turner pulled up at the blacksmith shop. "Hope Sundra's poked her head up out the ground by now. You guys go on ahead. I'll be along later."

Rob shook his head. "Sorry, Sergeant. The battalion needs you for an urgent mission first."

"Your Sundra isn't in, anyway," Aswan informed the pouting sergeant at arms. "She's out front, supervising the digging. She said they were her shovels, and she wasn't letting them out of her sight."

Turner grinned. "That's my woman. She loves her tools."

"She's planting a row of sunflowers all around the village wall," Aswan continued. "That way, if Dirt's sentries see us digging the moat, they'll think we are merely gardening."

Kim murmured approval.

Aswan smiled widely, revealing half a dozen gold teeth. "It was my idea." He ushered them to his shop and into his stronghold in back.

"Thank you for your hospitality," Rob said. "Can we trouble you to log on to the local area network? We need to broadcast a message."

"Happy to help, happy to help," the tradesman said importantly and did as he was asked.

Rob sat Turner down at the computer and told him what to type. He did, using two fingers in rapid fashion.

"Can I go now?" Turner half rose.

Jools pushed him back down. "Now we wait," he said. "To see if they take the bait."

Indeed, it wasn't long before a response came through the server:

<legs399> turning on yr friends so soon?

"It's Legs!" Turner whispered, as though the griefer could hear him on chat.

"Lead him on," Rob ordered, and the group crowded around to watch the screen.

Turner typed for a moment.

<kill4cash> u got better idea?
<legs399> come werk 4 r side

"Moron don't know how to spell," Turner muttered, typing again.

<kill4cash> whatz innit 4 me?
<legs399> = cut of loot

Everyone watched to see what Turner would do.

<kill4cash> deal

Turner made a face and waved his hands to indicate that he was lying.

<legs399> meet us at gate, dusk
<kill4cash> 10-4

The server indicated that Legs had left the game.

"*Now* can I go?" Turner begged his captain.

Rob wasn't certain he wanted the mercenary off unsupervised. But duty leave was good for morale. "Sixty minutes," he said. "No more. Everyone. Meet back here at curfew. We need to craft supplies."

When they had gone, Rob remained behind with Colonel M.

"You handled that quite well," the veteran praised his protégé.

Rob balled his fists with worry. "I'm just not sure we can trust that guy."

"One can never be sure of anything." Colonel M lowered his voice. "I'll let you in on a little secret, Captain: I don't know diddly about strategy."

Rob stopped his fidgeting.

"I know barely more than that about horses," he continued, and then he gave Rob a long look. "What I *do* know about is men." He dipped his giant brow. "Once you get a handle on human nature, you'll need nothing more to win a war."

"You mean, motivation is more important than preparation?"

"You can train all you want," the colonel said. "But in the heat of battle, the loyalty of your men is ten times more powerful than skill or weapons."

"I can't force Turner to follow orders, though."

"That is not your job. You must make him want to follow orders."

Rob thought about this advice as he waited for his troops to return.

*

Anticipation and stress rose like mercury in a thermometer as the sun began its descent. Rob was getting used to the day/night cycle that inevitably increased the need for offensive or defensive melees just as his energy waned. Perhaps that perverse readiness was what made Frida, Stormie, and Turner appear so capable all the time. It was as though they could jump up from a nap, slay a dragon, and settle right back into a sound sleep.

The girls returned first, bringing food from the farmer's cart and butcher shop. Jools sidled in with extra gunpowder and set up a brewing stand and cauldron. Rob and Colonel M helped him turn base potions into massive amounts of fire-resistance splash potions, which they intended to use on village structures to avoid another big burn. Everyone watched the clock as sixty minutes ticked by and Turner had yet to show up.

I should never have given him leave, Rob scolded himself. The line between motivation and manipulation was thin. To complicate matters, the battalion members had given their sergeant at arms the gems and ores they had mined to exchange for new armor. *Another mistake.*

At two minutes past curfew, Turner walked in the door, whistling.

"You're late, Sergeant!" Rob pointed out, though he was secretly very relieved.

"You'll thank me—Sundra sure did," Turner said smugly, tossing him a new helmet and chest plate from his inventory. He did the same for the others, making sure that Kim received the pink-dyed set.

"There isn't much time left," Rob said, laying out the sticks they still had and the feathers that Turner had procured from the fletcher. "We'll want some arrows to use on the griefers, assuming they don't fall for the moat."

Battalion Zero used the short time left to fill their food bars, test out their armor, and craft bows and ammunition. Aswan sat in the corner with the horses, watching Kim dress them in armor. They had to be ready to move out whenever the opportunity arose.

"Must you leave so soon, my angel?" Aswan asked the horse master.

"I have to see to my ranch—whatever's left of it," the petite, pink girl replied, feeling a pang of longing mixed with fear.

Aswan understood that Dr. Dirt's reach was long, and that without the help of the battalion, it might well encircle all of the Overworld. In fact, the very fate of the village could be decided within the next few hours.

"I will bide my time, sweet pickle." He sighed.

Rob paid closer attention to how Turner crafted his arrows this time. It struck him that perhaps full stacks of arrows might not be the best thing to entrust the mercenary with. But then he remembered Colonel

M's suggestion and vowed to work harder at drawing his worker bee with nectar.

When their inventories were bulging and the horses were enjoying their dinner, the troopers went back outside to wait for dusk. The sun seemed to be burning more brightly just before it retired for the day. As the flame-orange orb hung on the horizon, Stormie approached Rob for a quiet word.

"I want to . . . thank you," she said, intimately enough that he took a step back.

"You're welcome. For what?" He swallowed the lump in his throat.

"For sticking with us. You'd have every dang reason not to." She gazed at his face as though memorizing it, like a map. "I know this ain't your fight."

His greatest wish was to leave this world, and she knew it. But, suddenly, a truth hammered on his brain. "Maybe it doesn't matter which world I'm from," Rob said. "I'm just human, same as you. Your world *is* my world."

"At least for now," she said.

Yearning filled Rob—yearning for home, for answers, for this strong woman. He teetered between the need to be a commander and the need to just be himself for a change. His self-discipline stretched as taut as the tightwire he was balanced on. But there was still a thread of it left.

"Maybe someday, Stormie. . . ." He trailed off.

She caught her breath. "Someday . . . what?"

He straightened, looking quite the part of the dashing officer in his new armor. "Maybe someday this war will be over, and we'll find out who we really are."

She pulled away from him, sighing. "Maybe."

In the distance they heard shouting, and the one-two trudge of zombies on the move. Rob gave Stormie a wary smile. "See you on the other side, Artilleryman."

"Right on." She snapped off a salute.

Life sped up, as it always seemed to at dusk in the Overworld. This time, Rob was ready for it. The moat had been dug, the iron golem had been stationed, and the villagers lined the parapet, out of sight, awaiting the signal to toss the splash potions over the side.

As the sunlight dropped to an acceptable level, Dr. Dirt's legions lurched into the open.

"This is it, guys!" Frida rallied her battalion mates.

"All for one!" Kim cried.

"All for one," Stormie echoed. She eyed Turner and said through her teeth, "Right, Meat?"

He seemed wounded at her doubt. "'Course," he said, just as Dr. Dirt's nails-on-chalkboard voice hurtled across the plains.

"People . . . of . . . this village!"

"Yeah, yeah, we know," Jools said to the others, tiring of the griefer's arrogant manner. "'Throw out your . . . everything, or else I'll . . . blah, blah, blah.'" Jools motioned with his hands that he wished the griefer would just get on with it.

But Dirt continued, demanding their riches and threatening annihilation. Then he said, "The one they call . . . Turner! Come out! And you . . . will . . . not be harmed."

Rob's eyes drilled into the mercenary's back.

Turner rose and leaned over the top of the wall. "Never!" he yelled.

Now Legs stepped around the phalanx of zombies waiting for the order to attack. "Traitor!" He stomped his three feet. "We had a deal!"

"Why don't you take that up with the iron golem!" Turner replied.

As Legs waved an arm at the advance guard of zombies, the villagers sprang up and began dousing their homes and gate with fire resistance potion. Its effect would be temporary. Hopefully, the protection would hold long enough for the moat to capture the oncoming enemy.

Rob and his troops kept bows and arrows at the ready. They observed their attackers from the village wall, holding their ground as the shambling line of zombies fell back to reveal a platoon of armored skeletons. These began firing flaming arrows at the wooden gate and at the iron golem, which had been chained in position so it wouldn't wander ahead into the moat.

A deafening mob noise rose and fell in a tide of moans and bone clatters. Rob and the colonel watched as Legs and several other griefers crept behind their troops to place three mine carts on a track they had built that led toward the village and then off to the south. "They must be planning to haul away the village loot!" Rob said.

The marching skeletons were almost in range to crest the wall with their arrows. At Legs's command, the zombie ranks closed in behind them. Then, as the skelemob looked up to sight their arrow trajectories, their marching feet broke through the woolen wrap that disguised the moat. Instantly they dropped as one, crashing to the pit bottom, four layers down. Sundra's diggers had excavated the heck out of the trench, not stopping until they reached unbreakable bedrock.

This kept the skeletons who were still able to move from climbing out of the moat. Nothing kept the brain-dead zombies from falling into it, not even Legs's panicked screaming. Once again, a carefully crafted plan had fooled the griefer army into submission.

Then the battalion got their first brief glimpse of Dr. Dirt himself: a heavyset block of a man that belied his reedy voice, climbing into the first mine cart. Legs caught hold of the side of the cart and pushed, getting a three-legged running start. As the cart took off, he jumped in, shaking his fist at the villagers and members of Battalion Zero. Dirt's underlings followed in a hurry.

An enormous cheer erupted as the citizens realized that their antagonists had fled in defeat. The sound warred with the muffled groans and screeches that came from those trapped in the moat that were still alive.

"Don't open that gate!" Kim reminded her village friends. "Not until after sunup."

Rob asked her to assemble the townspeople so he could address them. He stood on a decorative planter block and called out, "This victory will only make Dr. Dirt angry and more determined to harm you. Now that we have provoked him, we intend to attack him with everything we've got." Concerned murmurs came from the crowd. "It looks as though he's fled to the extreme hills. If we can overthrow him there, this biome and six others will be free for good." Rob let this sink in. "We're asking for volunteers to act as reinforcements."

The crowd of villagers—and the other battalion members—reacted with surprise.

"Those of you who are willing and able, we can provide you with weapons and training," Rob promised, catching the colonel's eye and smiling. "Now, who's with me?"

For a moment, no one said anything. Then another cheer rose, and scores of villagers came forth to volunteer. Jools and Kim were charged with signing them up and preparing them to head out the next day. They would drill at Kim's ranch.

Frida and Stormie ran up and hugged Rob, one on either side.

"Good going, Captain!"

"Way to recruit!"

Turner stood there somewhat sourly, watching his commanding officer get all the female attention.

Rob reluctantly shrugged the girls off and called to him, "And, Sergeant! I'm promoting you. From now on you'll be Sergeant Major. And the new troops will answer to you."

You could have knocked Turner over with his own fletching.

He swiftly recovered, though. "Yes, *sir!*" he said, raising a hand in salute.

Colonel M saw the gesture and mouthed at his protégé, *I told you so.*

Rob grinned. For the first time since falling into the ocean, he felt truly buoyant.

CHAPTER 16

BATTALION ZERO LED THE NEW RECRUITS across the plains toward their training grounds. The sun sat high in the sky when they arrived at Kim's ranch the next day. Rob remembered the peaceful scene that had drawn him initially—the tidy stable yard, the comfortable box stalls, and the well-kept fencing in a sea of green prairie, dotted with buttery sunflowers. There it all was, still standing, still vibrant . . . except for the groans of undead horses coming from the stable.

Kim's shock had long since worn off, but anticipating the sight of the four-legged monsters now sent her into a panic, air whistling through her pursed lips. She shook so hard in the saddle that Nightwind took off for the paddocks at a gallop. Not wanting her to face the spectacle alone, Rob set Saber after her.

But the neatly divided paddocks held no zombied animals. Kim's horses stood huddled together watching the approaching strangers. Kim's and Rob's hopes rose, until they noticed that the adjoining pastures lay empty . . . except for distinct piles of burnt and rotting flesh. The zombie horses that Dr. Dirt and company had left outdoors had disintegrated in the bright sun!

Kim and Rob quickly wheeled Nightwind and Saber around and headed for the enclosed barn. Ungodly whinnies and neighs filled the air along with a sickening odor.

"Leave our mounts outside!" Kim warned. "The zombie horses will bust through the walls to attack them."

She and Rob snuck inside just far enough to see the mottled green coats and unfocused eyes of the affected equines. Kim sagged to the ground, ashen, and Rob scooped her up and pulled her back outside, just as the rest of the battalion rode in with Colonel M floating behind them.

"There are so many of them—" Kim's voice broke.

"How many, exactly?" the colonel asked.

Rob ducked back in and returned with the count.

"And Vanguard Frida," M continued. "How many apples have we?"

She pointed to a full stack, casting him a searching glance.

The colonel grew more urgent. "Quartermaster! How much gold?" They had mined quite a bit back at the old abandoned dig and had both blocks and ingots in their inventories. "Quickly! A crafting table," the old ghost demanded. He whispered something to Jools, who dipped into his brewing inventory while the colonel crafted away.

Kim watched, hope slowly replacing the horror in her eyes.

At last Colonel M said, "Let's give it a go." He nodded for Kim, Jools, and Rob to follow him inside. No one wanted to be that close to the flesh-eating monsters, but they knew they had to rise to the task.

"Quartermaster! You first!"

Jools pelted the distressed beasts with splash potions of weakness.

"Now the apples!"

The colonel had used the mined blocks and refined ingots to craft golden apples, some of them enchanted. "This worked on villagers once," he explained. "Let's hope it does the job now!"

They tossed the golden apples through the iron bars, and the trapped zombie horses wolfed them down. As the group watched, their groaning turned to hissing, their writhing turned to shuddering. Little by little, their coat colors faded and rejuvenated. Their passionless eyes reanimated. In a few minutes, each of the stabled animals had turned back into a true *equus ferus caballus*—a real, live horse.

Rob had never seen Kim so ecstatic. The color had come back into her pink cheeks and the spring had returned to her step. "Starla! Josie! Mister Wiggles!" They whinnied back at her. She unlatched one of the stall doors and entered, cooing, "Josie, Josie . . . I missed you so much."

Now Turner and Stormie crept through the barn door to witness the happy scene. Kim's joy spread to the rest of the group, and Stormie found herself hugging Turner. Rob, Jools, and Frida crowded around the colonel to rave about what his idea had accomplished.

"Who knew?" Frida said. "Colonel, you had just the right prescription for those sick horses."

Kim led Josie out of the barn. "I've used golden apples to encourage breeding, but I'm not much of a brewer. I had no idea that you could combine a weakness potion and a golden apple to cure a zombie horse. That's a valuable fact for my files."

Colonel M smiled at her. "A good horse master never stops learning." He turned to Rob. "Captain, don't let this one get away."

Rob promised he wouldn't, and Stormie glared at Kim jealously. She had nothing to worry about, though. Kim had been a good friend from day one, and she was a fellow horse lover, but she would always put her animals first. *Once a horse geek, always a horse geek,* Rob thought.

*

In the days that followed, horses and men stayed foremost in the cavalry commander's mind. Trusting to Colonel M's counsel, Rob realized that arms and ammunition could be considered secondary weapons. He needed to figure out the best way to use his officers to rally the new recruits and set a strategy for winning back the extreme hills boundaries.

One by one, Rob called his battalion members aside to chat.

"Frida, thanks for coming." He pointed her to a seat in his makeshift office that he'd converted from a horse stall.

The olive-hued survivalist sat on the edge of the wood block. "What's up, Newbie?"

"I want your take on how best to scout out the battle lines and site our attack."

This new Rob was still a surprise to Frida. He had moved from the blank slate she had encountered back on the beach to a real commander-in-the-making. Their meeting had been fortunate. She only wished she could help him more in his quest to get home . . . but that seemed beyond her power.

"I'm glad you asked," she said, returning to the topic at hand. "Getting a bead on Dirt's coordinates in the extreme hills will be tricky. As Colonel M said, there are lots of opportunities for ambush, and that doesn't bode well for spying. I'm thinking the only way to do it is to go undercover."

"You mean . . . infiltrate them?"

She nodded.

What a gutsy girl, Rob thought. Luckily, her confidence came from skill, not bravado.

"I know I can count on you, Vanguard. It's a perilous mission. I'll give you whatever help you need. Check in with me in a day or two."

She nodded again.

"And Frida . . . I appreciate . . . everything."

He asked her to call Turner in from where he was drilling troops.

Rob's conversation with his sergeant major showed less sentiment. Turner was riding high on a wave of self-importance.

"I've gotta say, Captain, I never thought you'd amount to much. And here you are holding your own alongside the guy who's commanding all the village troops! I've got those privates eating out of my hand." Turner plopped down on the wooden block uninvited.

"Have a seat, Sergeant Major," Rob said dryly. "I'll need both a weapons report and a division report. Have you managed to separate the company into three squadrons?"

"Done and done, sir," Turner replied, uncharacteristically focused on his task.

Rob marveled that the more you asked of some people, the more they could do. "Good. Then let's start arming the villagers to provide our cavalry front line with various degrees of protection. Take those with the best aim and give them bows. The biggest and strongest get swords. And the rest will use axes."

"Dirt won't know what hit him," Turner assured Rob. "We're two-thirds of the way through crafting two weapons apiece. Ammo, not so much. We're working on stockpiling land mines, though, besides as many arrows as we can make." Turner frowned. "I keep having to throw them out and start over."

"It's hard to meet your standards, I'm sure. But we don't have the luxury of perfection this time. Step up production, Sergeant Major," Rob ordered.

"Affirmative," Turner replied.

As long as he included the mercenary in the dialogue, Rob noted, he quit dragging his heels. *Thank you, Colonel M,* he said silently.

Knowing that Jools would have the skinny on their potion inventory, he dismissed Turner and asked him to summon the quartermaster to the stable.

*

While Jools hung at the door, waiting to be ushered in, Rob recalled their first confrontation. Jools was thinking about the same thing.

"Sorry about that pufferfish," Jools said with a wry grin, accepting the seat when Rob offered it.

"I thought I was dying," Rob admitted. Jools's great talent was to think outside the box at just the right moment, a valuable skill. "What were the odds of someone catching a poisonous fish in their mouth?"

"But it worked," Jools said, and the two reminisced briefly about that fishing trip. "I'd like to do some more fishing before we leave the plains," Jools said. "You never know what kind of loot I might dredge up. Isn't that how you found Turner?"

Rob laughed. "Nah, the cat dragged him in. But seriously, Jools. We're going to need you to run some computer simulations for different battle scenarios, starting with one of us infiltrating the enemy encampment. By the time Frida turns on the real griefers, it will be too late for them to retaliate. Or, at least, it had better be."

Even Jools was impressed with Frida's bold proposal. "She's a woman after my own heart," he said. "That's the kind of girl I could really hide behind."

Rob recalled the quartermaster's previous attempts to remain in the background. "Those days are gone, buddy," he said. "We need all the manpower we can get, and you're a good rider. Can you see your way clear to taking up arms?"

Jools hesitated, and embarrassment colored his pale face. "It's against my typical policy," he said, "but I'll make an exception this time for the good of the battalion."

Rob looked skeptical.

"You have my word," Jools added, to the captain's satisfaction.

They agreed that potions would be less effective in this battle, where the hazardous terrain would give Dr. Dirt the advantage. But boosting everyone's eyesight with night vision potion would be worthwhile.

"I'll get right on it, Rob. Sir." Jools wasn't used to meeting anyone whose powers of insight and deduction complemented his own. "And might I say that you're doing a bang-up job?"

"Right back at you," Rob said, shaking Jools's hand.

The remaining troopers also pledged their support. Stormie agreed to rig the mine carts they'd brought from the mesa with TNT. They could send them along Dirt's own tracks to detonate his supply stores.

She offered to lead out and act as vanguard when they reached the extreme hills, where her map would not be sufficient to gauge the terrain. Kim came charging into his office in a pink rage and volunteered to strike the first blow when the battle began.

"I can never forgive those griefers for what they did to my herd," she said, more fired up than Rob had ever seen her. "I want to make them pay."

Now she was sounding more like Turner than the bronc whisperer who had shown Rob up in the corral that first day. "Active duty doesn't relieve you of your horse master obligation," he reminded her.

"I can do both, sir!"

He gratefully accepted her among the cavalry guard and promoted her to corporal. She would act as liaison between Turner's infantry and the mounted officers. "Let's go tell him the good news," Rob said.

They approached Turner's squadrons, drilling on one of the side pastures under the watchful eye of Colonel M The villagers, who were used to roaming at will, when and where they wanted to go, were having a difficult time marching in unison. Turner screamed at them to act as a unit.

"Don't ya get it? Working together makes a team—and that there's stronger than any one guy," Rob heard him say. "That's how come a line of cavalry soldiers charges abreast, not single file." Turner noticed the captain's approach and ducked his head. "Now carry on," he blustered. "One, two, one, two . . ."

*

In a few days the preparations neared completion. Frida donned an old skin that Kim had up in her attic that they hoped would fool the griefer contingent. She set out on her lonely and dangerous operation. They would hear no more from her until she signaled them as they planned from lower coordinates on the extreme hills. Rob couldn't help wondering if he would see her green face again.

Before suiting up and moving toward the rendezvous point, Rob had to consult one more of his key players. After dinner, he strolled out to the pasture where Saber, Beckett, and Duff were dozing. Rob slipped through the gate and walked up to the black horse that had carried him so far.

"If this was a perfect world," the captain said to Saber, "I wouldn't rightly ask another thing of you." He scratched the horse's shoulder and received a low nicker in reply. "But, for now, I need you to give me just one more battle."

The man and mount stood together in companionable silence late into the night. Rob wished it would never end. Finally, he returned to the barn and the bedroll Kim had given him to replace the one he'd lost in the Nether. He wouldn't ever take sleeping in a bed for granted again.

He woke at first light to Colonel M's gentle nudge. "Is it time to go?" he asked fuzzily.

"It is for me," the wise man's head uttered. "I must retire to my summer home while you go take care of business."

Rob sat up, wide awake now. Apprehension knifed through him. *Why would the colonel leave just when they needed him most?*

"I can be of no use to you in a physical battle," his mentor explained. "I have already transmitted my small bit of knowledge, which you have interpreted well. Now it is time for you to put it into practice."

"But . . . how will we contact you to let you know the outcome?"

The bemused head drifted toward the stable door. "I have my ways of knowing," Colonel M said. "We shall meet again."

"I'll never forget you," Rob promised. He wanted to tell the colonel that he had been nothing before they'd met—that he was a fence-riding cowboy, not a leader. He wanted to list his shortcomings and insist that he wasn't fit to start a revolution. But he knew that the colonel would want him to turn all those negatives into positives and to hurl them at the enemy with all his might.

As Rob wrestled with these thoughts, he watched his mentor's head grow fainter and more transparent, until all he could see was the half-empty hay net on the opposite stable wall.

*

"Move out!" Rob called a few hours later to Battalion Zero and its infantry reinforcements. Stormie took the lead on Armor, as usual, ponying Ocelot behind them. It felt strange not to see Frida riding ahead of Jools and Beckett, and odder still not to hear Turner's banter. Rob had relegated the sergeant major and his corporal to the rear of the foot soldier ranks. He felt better about trusting Turner to hold steady in the rearguard with Kim there to watch over him.

He cast a final glance behind him and was pleased to see the rows of villagers marching smartly along. There was, of course, no way to hide the fact that they meant to strike at Dr. Dirt's forces. Rob hoped that having Frida embedded in their unit would pay off with crucial intelligence and well-placed booby traps.

"So, Captain Rob," Jools said as they rode beside each other, "which battle option have you selected?"

The strategist had run probability figures for the three most likely scenarios.

"We'll stick with Dirt's own battle plan and turn it against him," Rob replied. "The man has used the same configuration every time. All we have to do is anticipate it."

Jools nodded. "Pick off the skelemobs, skirmish with the zombies, and blast 'em with TNT whenever possible."

"The griefers don't have Kim's zombie horses anymore," Rob pointed out, "so we'll have the upper hand."

"Sounds like a shoo-in," Jools said.

Turner relayed the orders to his infantry. "Squadron One will return skeleton arrow fire. Squadron Two will move in with their blades, followed by Squadron Three to clean up any baby zombies, chicken jockeys, or retreating griefers. Case closed."

Rob had dropped back to make sure the entire band understood the battle plan. "In the event of unforeseen . . . events," he announced, "we'll sound the retreat. Remember, this is *our* fight, not one you picked. If it all goes south . . . you people get out of there and don't look back."

Turner eyed him incredulously. "Turn and run?" he stage-whispered at Rob. "That's your fallback? That ain't the way I'd do it."

"Think about it, Sergeant Major," the captain said. "That leaves them alive for another attempt."

Turner knew that Dr. Dirt wouldn't give up until he was no more, but the mercenary did not wish to endorse any strategy that didn't end with more loot in the bank. "Well, what do I know?" he muttered when Rob didn't change his mind. "I'm just meat."

CHAPTER 17

THE BATTALION RODE DUE SOUTH AND PICKED up Dr. Dirt's mine cart tracks as they skirted the village. It made for easy navigation to the battlefront. Once again, Battalion Zero's officers were on edge.

"Hills, ho, Captain!" called Stormie from her lead post on Armor.

Before them spread a biome like none Rob had seen. The ground cover seemed to have been brushed with turquoise, and the rocky hills rose toward the clouds in dizzying terraces. Every angle offered variety. As they rounded a bend, they saw a sheer cliff face smiling into a deep-blue pool, and around the next, a grove of oak trees rising from a prominent ridge. The sight line at the top would be unobstructed for a thousand kilometers, Rob realized with a thrill.

He could scarcely believe he was laying eyes on the fabled land—the extreme hills. His longing for home hit him like a hurricane. From what he'd learned about this world, if he could locate his original spawn point, he might be able to respawn on command into his previous realm. He could practically hear the cattle lowing and taste that rare steak cooked over an open fire.

The mine cart tracks began to climb once they crossed over from the plains to the foothills. Saber grunted a bit as he worked harder on the incline but did not slacken his pace. When they arrived at the spot Stormie had marked on the map, they halted. There they would wait until late afternoon, when Frida would use a glass reflector and the sun's rays to signal them in code.

Rob sent for his sergeant major at arms and corporal. "Turner, designate an alternate second-in-command to direct your troops. We'll need all riders at the front."

"Let me at them!" Kim cried.

"Easy, Corporal," Rob said. "Let's not get overexcited."

"That's *my* job," Turner added.

All of the advance guard donned armor, and Kim outfitted the horses, who pawed at the ground, sensing her urgency. Jools and Stormie scoured the hillside for unnatural flashes of light.

Suddenly Stormie spotted something blinking. She pointed toward a shaded area. "Look!"

Jools brought out his computer to translate the code. He sighed loudly. "She's in. She's safe!" He paused, watching the reflected pulses of sunlight. "She's placed trip wires to the west, at our direct approach. Dirt will see us coming and his legions will walk right into them!" He paused again. "Take down these rendezvous coordinates, Stormie."

She recorded them on her map and prepared to lead the cavalry to them. "Won't Frida be glad to see Ocelot again?" she remarked.

Turner offered to lead the horse through the steep terrain so Stormie could focus on their course. As the sun began to drop behind the surrounding foothills, Jools made the rounds with night vision potion.

"No crowding, now. Some for everyone," he said, doling out the potent drink among the cavalry and infantry, and pouring good measures down the horses' throats.

Every hair on Saber's coat seemed to stand on end, Rob noticed, as the black horse danced in place. "Mount up!" he cried, to prevent himself from second-guessing the whole plan. He wasn't sure what the order was for setting foot soldiers in motion, so he drew on his old roundup vocabulary. "Head 'em up . . . move 'em out!"

The villagers responded with shrill war whoops that bounced through the rugged terrain. Their objective was to make as much noise as possible to ensure that the griefers would see them coming.

Turner let loose a loud, adrenaline-fueled rant, largely aimed at his nemesis. "Ready or not, Legs, here we come! I'ma tear you limb from limb from limb!" He urged Duff forward at a gallop, with Ocelot flying beside them. "No one takes over the world without Sergeant-Major Turner's say-so!" They passed Rob and Kim on Saber and Nightwind.

"That first shot's mine!" Kim yelled at Turner.

He cut her a tender look. "Can't let you do that. Battalion Zero, this one's for you!" He pressed Duff and Ocelot into overdrive, passing Stormie on Armor, and raced straight for the TNT trip wires.

Down from the hills came the familiar uproar of the undead, the echoes increasing their clamor: "Uuuuh-*uh-uh-uh* . . . oooh-*oh-oh-oh* . . . !"

Then the battalion could see the green masses sweeping across the hillside toward the traps. *Kerblammm!* The first land mine exploded as Turner rushed forward to attack. Rob had no choice but to veer off to the north, leaving his sergeant major as a decoy, as he led the infantry out of trap range himself. Then the rest of the cavalry pulled even with him, making for the rendezvous with Frida.

The villagers shouted behind them, and monsters groaned ahead. Rob rode forward in Saber's saddle, his ears filling with the sound of clattering hooves and the huffing of horse breath as they climbed and climbed and climbed. Mid-gallop, he noticed something was missing.

"Jools!" he called to the quartermaster, who ran beside him on Beckett. "Listen! No bones!"

The characteristic rattle was absent from the din. The monstrous groans grew louder, accompanied by the clanking of iron.

"Sounds like they've augmented their zombie forces! And they're armored!"

They hadn't reckoned on this. They were riding into a melee in which their bows and arrows would be useless.

Still, the horses climbed, nearing Frida's hiding spot.

"I see her!" Stormie shouted, just as Turner, Duff, and Ocelot came into view from the other route.

Frida had torn off her griefer disguise, but had no time to wriggle into chainmail. She caught Ocelot's reins when Turner tossed them and vaulted into the saddle the way Kim had taught her back at the ranch. The six riders pulled up to regroup while more blasts punctuated the air.

"Vanguard!" Rob called. "Report."

Frida's dark-green face shined with sweat. "Their zombie numbers are huge, and they're heavily armed. Dirt is calling this 'Operation Doomsday'!" She waved in one direction. "My trip wires won't hold them off for long, Captain." She waved the other way. "But up there's the viewpoint you were looking for."

Rob caught his breath, surveying the area. Hand-to-hand combat would be deadly here, where the steep terraces provided no cover and greater risk of falling. They might be able to hold the hilltop, but getting there would be nearly impossible.

On came the enemy troops across the slope, with Dr. Dirt's unmistakable screech echoing behind them. "Battalion . . . Zero-*oh-oh* . . . ! This—is your day . . . to die-*ie-ie*!"

A swarm of zombies hurtled at the group. "Battalion: Attack!" Rob cried, sending Saber forward.

Turner pulled his sword out and savagely hacked at the moving undead. With their protective gear, it took blow after blow to slow them, let alone subdue them. Stormie, Kim, and Jools followed the sergeant major's lead, slicing and dicing until they removed enough limbs to score a kill. But to Rob's alarm, each death spawned twice or four times as many green ghouls, each one materializing fully equipped and extremely angry.

"They're closing in! What should we do, Captain?" Turner puffed in between passes with his blade, sending still-writhing green flesh every which way. Behind them, the villagers charged, their whoops interspersed with screams as they took hits or tumbled into the rocks.

The smart thing to do would be to ride down toward a clearing or to an area where they could lure the zombies over a cliff. If they did that, though, they might never make it back up to the viewpoint Frida had located. Rob felt torn in two. One part of him was committed to the safety and success of the battalion, the other was stubbornly determined to find his way home. He knew what he *should* do. . . .

"Battalion, to that hilltop. Follow me!" He clapped his heels against Saber's sides and sent him scrabbling for the viewpoint.

*

Fortunately, the climb slowed the zombies' advance and was too steep for baby zombies or chicken jockeys to attempt. The villagers' third squadron used their stone and iron axes to mow the chicken jockeys down like weeds, while the second unit tried to hold off the larger monsters with their swords. Meanwhile, the first squadron and Rob's cavalry guard found themselves only able to flee toward high ground—their arrows could not penetrate the undead's body armor.

"This ain't how I pictured it, Captain!" Stormie called through gritted teeth as Armor tore up the hillside, leaving the odor of rotting flesh below them.

"Nothing's for certain in war time," Rob answered.

A chorus of screams rose behind them as the onrushing mob overcame a cluster of villagers, some of them becoming zombies and turning on their own squadron.

Frida threw a desperate glance over her shoulder, and Ocelot hesitated.

"Keep going!" Jools yelled. "It's our only chance."

All of a sudden an amplified voice addressed them from the high end of the scale. "Battalion . . . Zero! Hope you . . . *admire* . . . the view!" And Dr. Dirt unleashed a hideous cackle.

From their greater elevation, they could see more villagers being taken down by decomposing green limbs.

"Cap'n!" Turner shoved Duff over toward Saber. "My men are taking an awful beating."

"And this hillside is unstable," Kim added. "The horses could lose their footing at any moment!"

But it was too late to alter their course. The only way to succeed now—and to get a clear view of the horizon—would be to amass all their power on the hilltop and battle their way back through Dirt's ranks.

Rob ignored Turner and Kim and galloped on. His enhanced night vision now matched the horses' normal eyesight in low light. He and Saber twisted and turned as one, navigating the hillside terraces like reverse moguls. They finally burst above the tree line, onto an open plateau, gasping for breath in the clear air. If Frida was right, Rob would be able to see all the way across four biomes and out to sea.

Just as he drew Saber to a halt to get his bearings, another ominous noise brought his body to attention. The rhythmic clack of marching bones approached, sounding like a hundred men shaking bags of bricks. *Now the skelemobs are out?* Rob thought, realizing his earlier assumption about Dr. Dirt's plan was wrong.

As if on cue, the evil griefer commander stepped out into the open among his undead troops and barked into his redstone-powered megaphone: "And this . . . I must see . . . *for myself!*"

"Rob!" Turner motioned with his chin in the doctor's direction.

"I'm on it!" Rob yelled, reining Saber off to the side. With his super night vision, Rob drilled his gaze at Dr. Dirt, and the horse instantly knew where his rider wanted him to go. But four diamond-armored zombies guarded the griefer.

It was time to fight fire with . . . hotter fire. Trusting Saber to continue to charge, Rob rooted about in his inventory, finally producing one of the enchanted golden apples that Colonel M had crafted. When he drew his sword, it achieved Overpowered status. Anything he touched with it would instantly die!

He and Saber bore down on the knot of fortified zombies, which snarled and waved, dropping limbs and chunks of flesh. Believing himself safe, their commander stood calmly behind them.

"So! Cap-tain!" Dirt yelled. "We . . . meet . . . a . . ."

At Rob's nudge, Saber collected himself and sprang, clearing the zombies with his leap and landing so close to Dr. Dirt that the griefer's wide, black eyes looked like obsidian blocks. One downward slash was all it took to split the griefer squarely in two.

As the halves of Dr. Dirt fell sideways, Rob finished, "We meet again." He pulled Saber back a step to feast his eyes on the already-decaying lumps. "Only this time," Rob growled, "you're dead!"

His victory was short-lived. Over the sharp rise swarmed a jittering line of armored skeletons. He wheeled Saber and headed back to his mounted unit, accompanied by recognizable shouts from Legs and another raspy voice that they had not heard in quite some time.

"Battalion Zero!" came the rumbling call. "Your pitiful efforts have made me stronger!"

Frida threw a frightened glance at Turner. Kim and Jools exchanged stares.

"Who is it?" Rob called to Stormie.

"It . . . can't be. But it is!" she said. "It's Lady Craven!"

The griefer sorceress was hidden by a wall of oncoming skeletons, their helmeted skulls bobbing hideously.

"I told you I could not be killed!" Lady Craven declared. "I gain health from every one of my legions that you vanquish, and Dr. Dirt was worth more than the rest put together. Now you will never stop me from overtaking the Overworld."

"Then you shoulda sent more at us than a bunch of fall-apart zombies!" Turner taunted.

"This is *their* hill," Lady Craven shouted. "They wear enchanted diamond armor, and their skeletons will kill any one of you that challenges their sovereignty."

"I think she's bluffing," whispered Stormie.

"Me, too!" yelled Kim, launching Nightwind at the approaching skelemob.

Stormie took off after her, drawing her bow and preparing to give cover.

Just then, three skeleton snipers let fly three arrows, which by very steep odds, hit their mark. That mark was Stormie.

The triad of arrows lodged together in the adventurer's throat, knocking her off Armor. She hit the ground hard and rolled out of the way of Nightwind's hooves. Rob and Turner reached her first, followed closely by Jools and Frida. Kim pulled up and doubled back just in time to see Rob jump from Saber and take Stormie in his arms.

Frida and Turner pulled their bows and held off the skeletons. Rob's face froze as he watched blood pour from Stormie's throat, the light in her night-visioned eyes fading.

"We . . . can't win, Captain," Stormie whispered. "I . . . tried."

"Stormie, hold on," Rob willed her. "Jools! Don't you have something—?"

But Stormie's health bar was dwindling.

"Rob . . ."

"*Ssh!* Save your strength!"

". . . promise me . . ."

"Anything, Stormie."

She clutched at his arm. "Promise you'll . . . go now. S-surrender . . ."

He shook his head fiercely.

"You . . . must," she implored him. "Live to fight . . . another day." She hiccuped.

He shook his head hopelessly.

She was gone.

"Hold 'em off, Jools!" Turner threw Jools his bow and jumped down from Duff, but he was too late.

The mercenary reached over and felt Stormie's neck for a pulse, then let go. He gently removed the arrows that had caused the fatal blow, shooting a stricken look at his captain. "These . . . these was mine." He held out the finely fletched arrows that must have been retrieved by the skeleton archers.

Again, Lady Craven's voice fell upon their ears like the rumble of loose cannons: "We have you surrounded, Battalion Zero! Give up!"

*

"It should've been me!" Kim said tearfully to her compatriots.

"Or me," Turner whispered gruffly.

Rob had gone cold inside. It had been his choice that led them into this mess. His choice that got Stormie—

Her words floated back to him. Threatening moans and creaking bones ringed the small battalion in a sea of hostility. The innocent villagers faced similar peril a short way down the hillside. All would be lost if Rob didn't take Stormie's advice.

He drew a deep breath. "Corporal! Sound the retreat."

Kim rose to comply, but Turner put out a hand. "I'll do it," he said. He gave three long whoops and two short ones, waited a moment, and repeated the call. A relieved cry rose from the released villagers, and the cavalry officers heard them crashing down the hillside as fast as they could run.

"But . . . where do we go?" Kim asked.

Rob didn't have an answer. He glanced at Jools, but the quartermaster shrugged.

Frida hadn't been a survivalist all her life for nothing. Although the loss of her friend was destroying her inside, if they didn't move, they'd all follow Stormie to the grave, the Void, or whatever fate awaited them.

"This way!" she said to the group, pointing straight up to the summit.

It was too dangerous to ask the horses to carry them. They dismounted and led them, Frida tugging the now riderless Armor upward, with the sounds of the mob not far behind them.

"We'll never be able to fend them off from up there," Turner argued. "It'll be a feeding frenzy!"

"How do you think I found this viewpoint?" Frida countered. "I noticed it on my way to hide a Nether portal."

"A Nether portal!" Rob exclaimed. "I didn't order that."

"For times of need," she emphasized. "You couldn't have known, Newbie. And if we didn't need it, you wouldn't have known."

They came upon a stone block room with an open door.

"*Surrender, Battalion Zero . . . !*" Lady Craven insisted, as she and her grotesque legions came ever closer.

"We'll use the Nether to travel to an outpost biome," Frida said. "Somewhere they won't try to find us! It's something Stormie would've done," she added.

Kim and Jools nodded. Rob could see that she was right.

"Uh-uh!" Turner said, gripping Duff's reins stubbornly. "I ain't the type to give in. I'll fight to the death!"

Rob eyed the mercenary and realized he had two choices: give him an order, or make him want to follow one.

"I hear there's money to be made in the ice plains. Outlaws with big loot that needs guarding . . . or borrowing."

Jools recognized his captain's tactic. "And not much chance of getting caught, either."

This interested Turner, but he cocked his head at the enemy lines. "My friend, Legs, has a date with destiny," he growled.

Frida caught his elbow. "He's under Lady Craven's wing now, Meat. And she's got all of Dr. Dirt's power, plus her own."

This, Turner couldn't deny.

Softly, Rob said, "Don't think of it as retreating. Think of it as regrouping. We'll make some money, reorganize, and ride on those griefers again."

Kim pressed her lips together. "I'm not giving up."

"Neither am I!" Rob said, and Jools and Frida nodded. "We'll—" His voice broke. "—live to fight another day." He dropped his gaze to stare at the ground.

For a moment, no one said anything.

"Well . . ." Turner offered. "If you put it that way . . ."

The ear-splitting shrieks, groans, and rattles meant that the zombies and their protectors were almost upon them.

"Come on!" Frida urged, and they entered the stone enclosure that held the Nether portal, pulling their horses along.

In his desperation, Rob felt one ray of hope. As long as his heart was still beating, he still had a chance to make it home. But now the needs of the many outweighed his greatest desire, to see his ranch again. He knew that to get there, he would have to liberate this world first.